Witches' Brew

Gregory John Ferris

By the same author:

Prologue

Dad was a matchmaker. My mother? Dead. The final four-letter word. If she had lived and he had died, perhaps she'd have performed better in the role. But then she was, you know, dead.

Put bluntly, Father was not up to the task. Other than his first marriage, his others were disasters. Cliché struck repeatedly and I ended up with various stepmoms who served their two-year stint before ennui set in for one or both of the spouses. I may be incorrect, but I seem to remember that they all wore the same perfume.

In school, I had been termed a quick learner. I assume that I inherited that particular trait from my late mother.

In college I enrolled in a STEM program, those where one studies either how to prolong life with drugs or how to destroy it with weapons.

Following a flush of failed marriages, Father drew a woman whose age lacked mine by a year to the day. Unthrilled by the prospect of ringing another cliche, I chose the adult route and ran away from home and school.

I tried all sorts of work, those restricted to the minimal of manual labor, for my privileged if pseudo-Oedipal life had taught me that fewer things made less sense than breaking a sweat. Intellectual endeavors were more attuned to my nature.

Panhandling I rationalized was arduous, akin to a hybrid of panning for gold and financial chess, a zero-sum game between a current cypher and one whose self-esteem would be raised by his, or her contribution to my wellbeing. I observed that young, likely unmarried couples were my most lucrative source of alms during my mendicant era.

Aside from my self-earnings, I was able to survive on the allowance that my father continued to disperse into my bank account, one augmented when, phoning me on my birthday, he learned that I was residing in London.

One day I found myself, no, not that way.

I simply found myself in a London library reading the story of the prodigal son. The cacophony of London was only a vague hum, interrupted intermittently by a distant siren. I finished the brief story, one obviously redacted, opened the possibility of a rapprochement in my future.

However much fabricated, I felt a sense of relief that I had last enjoyed back home in the New World. I relaxed and dozed off. For what was I at that moment other than an itinerant, by all appearances homeless and possibly deranged.

When I awoke, only a few minutes later, the story that I will here shortly include, begins.

I awoke to a quiet hum, similar to the drone of the London traffic outside, but so much closer and evidently loud enough to rouse me from my brief nap.

Except for the requisite silence of a library, it might have passed unnoticed. As soon as I took note of it, the sound stopped.

The machine sat there; small, elegant, silent. There was no glowing screen. It was menacing in its impossibility of existence and its unknown purpose. I suspected that I might be hallucinating.

I turned my head from side to side, all was normal in the library. The visitors ranged from the destitute to astute scholars. I positioned myself was somewhere in the bottom quartile.

My mine raced through possibilities. Despite my having missed breakfast I was not seeing things, certainly not a private toaster for a near homeless American. Moreover there was no scent of delicious freshly warmed and browned bread. My brief fixation on food passed as my curiosity mounted.

Upon closer inspection I wondered how anyone could have thought of a toaster as remotely likely. I can only surmise it must be due to the existence of a yet to be discovered nerve running from the eyes to the stomach.

How I could have entertained such a link is beyond comprehension. My mind raced for an answer, discovering and rejecting theories that grew more bizarre in the short minute that the machine was in my presence.

I say machine, but as I recall now, months later, I reflected then that it was more like an expensive toy from a bygone era. That idea struck me as logical enough for me to resume breathing. That was it, a toy. It was well crafted, but only a toy, a model of a real machine, whatever that was.

It resembled in many ways the large machines of the industrial age that I had recently seen in the British museum. the odd wooden handle and here and there appointments of red and black leather.

Was this device before me an exhibit on temporary loan from the museum? Something I overlooked here in library since I had observed so many similar items elsewhere? Had a librarian placed in before me as a not-so-subtle alarm clock, with an implied 'Time to leave, sir'?

I swiveled my head in an attempt to discover the prankster. The same visitors were my only suspects, and I freed them from accusation.

I returned to my toy.

Looking more closely at it, I thought how clever it was to have placed a book on the seat upholstered in crimson leather. Both the book and the leather appeared as fresh as yesterday.

I discovered later that the book was rarer than a first edition, it was as later scientific tests would prove, an only edition, a private printing of one.

What you are about to read is the story as it was delivered to me, the only change being one forced on me by my American publisher, who insisted on American English spelling. I'm sure Watson would not be amused.

CHAPTER 1 221b

I opened the door to our shared lodgings on the second floor of the narrow building we'd inhabited for several years. As I crossed the threshold, I was immediately attacked by a rapidly approaching unknown object. Quickly parrying the threat with a flick of my walking stick, I watched as it veered away. I recognized the offending object as a thick book and followed its now retreating trajectory as it narrowly missed a vase on the mantle before the tome came to rest, cover up, on the floor next to the fireplace.

"A more to the left, and you'd have had it in one", Holmes stated sardonically. "Consigned to the flames, where it belongs."

I stepped to the resting missile to glean its offensive origin. As I bent to read its title, a second pang of pain in my lower shoulder blade in as many minutes made its own unwelcome presence known, the first having stabbed me when I had twisted suddenly to avoid what I now realized was nothing more than the collected works of William Shakespeare.

"Really Holmes? I've never taken you for the most well-read of Englishmen, but neither have you struck me as a book burning Philistines."

"Setting fire to scrolls is a more apt insult for the period, as books," he began.

"Yes, yes", I interrupted. "To confine the Bard to flames would be criminal. This is a great work of literature," I stated as I retrieved the tome and placed it next to the vase.

1

"There, two masterpieces are now safely beyond your destructive grasp," I said firmly.

"It is art, not history, Watson. The past is a misremembered country. Alibis are not facts."

"Morose, sullen, you have much in common with the criminal class, Holmes."

"You are observant in your own specialty, Watson."

I passed over the compliment with an "Indeed."

Holmes nodded at the copy of MacBeth.

"The tale is a hybrid, unobservant witnesses, and with the passage of time it is mixed with recalcitrance to make the story less interesting and more royal. The play became a witch's brew of half-truths and poetic seasonings."

"Three witches, if I remember correctly," I said in an attempt to draw Holmes from his fugue.

"Holmes, you bring the criminal to bay and transfer fully and completely, your morosity and sullenness to your malignant quarry."

"I confess it all, Watson. Yet this metropolis remains calm for us. When shall the horn sound hunt? It is dreary. The superior criminals are holidaying in Brighton, and I've no taste to hunt them while they sit. Those that remain in London are the dregs, without interest."

I spread the tobacco smoke scented curtains to refute his description.

"Unlike this confinement, the sky is clear the wind a pleasant breeze. The sun shines benignly on a peaceful capital."

"Indeed," Holmes echoed politely, then retreated to his prepared position.

"All you say is true. I term it dreary."

Holmes stared at the outside world.

"Watson, when you must redo Macbeth, it is an abomination."

I let the storm pass. At times Holmes come resemble nothing so much than a bored child on a rainy day.

A moment later his clouds passed, and he perked up and stretched, like an awakening bird of prey.

"I do believe that our forecasts are on the verge of coinciding."

A knock sounded at the door, and I stepped across the room to answer the door, leaving Holmes to gaze at the passing traffic.

A ruddy faced man, thin, wearing a clean, fashionable but worn suit was standing in the hallway. I invited him in.

"I am sorry to arrive unannounced, Dr. Watson," then raised his voice on account of the outside sound coming in through the now open window, "and you Mr. Holmes, but I considered my matter urgent."

"And you are?" I asked.

He hesitated a moment before replying.

"George Herbert. I am sorry but it has been a dreadful morning."

"I appreciate the feeling," commiserated Holmes.

"What can we do to help you, Mr. Herbert?" Holmes asked, motioning to a chair for the sudden visitor.

Herbert glanced at the offered seat but declined with a single shake of his head.

"I need your help," he said, stating the obvious.

"I have a place, a workshop, in Kensington. A benefactor lets me use it without charge," he added in response to my inadvertent expression of surprise.

Kensington is an expensive neighborhood, an area that Herbert did not appear to be able to afford. But looks can be deceiving.

"I've been robbed gentlemen," and this time I controlled my reaction for he appeared to not be a man with the means to have been robbed.

"What has been stolen?" Holmes asked.

"My, my invention. From a locked workshop. I don't understand how. It was locked."

"Your benefactor?"

"He has no key and is nearly 90 years old and can barely walk."

"His caretakers?"

"They have no key. Like their ward, they are above reproach."

"The windows?" I ventured.

"They are much too small."

"As is this case," I said calmly.

"Let us not be hasty, for Mr. Herbert is in need of assistance."

Herbert nodded emphatically.

"Yes, I need help."

"You arrive suddenly, without notice and present us with a locked room mystery," Holmes said with a slight smile.

"Why this is an enigma worthy of a writer such as yourself Watson. My dear doctor, you promised, nay prescribed me excitement today. Let us investigate this piece of literary adventure in situ.

Herbert appeared embarrassed.

"I have very little money, I'm not sure...".

"No matter, Mr. Herbert. You have found two more benefactors on what was until now a dreadful, dreary London morning."

Our new, impoverished client left to wait for us downstairs as we gathered a few items.

"This man who introduced himself as Mr. Herbert," I began.

"You find it suspicious, Watson?"

"Not particularly. The name means nothing to me, and his demeanor is one of not having a shilling to spare. He admitted as much. I am one for charity, you know that with my medical work."

"Watson you are wealthy in generosity, no English doctor more so. As to our Mr. Herbert, he is rich in adventure and will spend it lavishly I wager."

"A missing steam engine or some such device, why is that of any interest. Have we sunk to chasing after lost cattle, and missing puppies? Your client's case is trivial and your cavalier acceptance of it, depresses me to the level of your own gloom of a scant twenty minutes ago. A brief time, but one I would not care to repeat."

"I must disagree Watson. This brief time has been the most illuminating in many months. This man, whom you so accurately described as having introduced himself as George Herbert is clearly desperate, yet uncertain that we can aid him. It is at the root of his desperation that I have confidence we will find the flower of adventure. Come Watson, the game's afoot."

CHAPTER 2 The Carriage House

Herbert roomed in a house and had use of the carriage house as the owner employs cabs exclusively.

"I suspect that he fears horses. He is a strange man, but I shan't complain. A bit of a hermit," Herbert explained to Holmes and myself.

Holmes responded "A large metropolis is bound to have its share of oddity and where else but in a crowd to excel as a hermit."

Surprisingly, the carriage house had electricity, and work benches filled with devices of unknown purpose, for such a man as Herbert apparently had various interests, and numerous gauges to measure who knows what.

"I survived on half ration for six months in order to have the wherewithal to have the electrical power installed. As for the monthly bill, I may resort to eating these," Wells said sardonically, pointing to his shoes while staring Holmes directly in the eyes.

"Money is neither my motivation nor my expectation in cases that interest me. Cases that, shall we say, are illuminating or electrifying."

Wells' laboratory reminded me of Holmes work room and chemistry experiments, and I was careful to touch nothing, and to keep a healthy distance for fear of static electricity.

Holmes proceeded to investigate every crook and nanny of the carriage house. When he had finished, he motioned us to a small work bench next to a grimy window.

"Well, I have completed my review but before we proceed, Watson, what do you conclude has happened here? It has been nearly 24 hours since Mr. Herbert noticed the theft."

I spoke.

"Once you have eliminated the impossible then the improbable, however unlikely must be true," I said triumphantly.

"It follows that the improbability is that it was never here, and you have your own reason for getting us here," I added.

"Excellent Watson. Pray continue."

"You were and are bored and this is a prank for my upcoming birthday. I expect that in the main house an early dinner is being prepared in my honor, along with other festivities."

"If only if that were true. You will need to be content with a show and dinner in a modest restaurant with I fear, no fanfare. You have however the scent and search the correct trail."

Hebert stood by, interested in our dialogue but visibly impatient for a resolution.

"Let me introduce you not to George Herbert, but young Mr. Herbert George Wells."

Wells bowed slightly.

"Watson, Mr. Wells is a man known well enough publicly to warrant a small article, and photo in the Times, yet who decided to disguise crudely his name from the world's greatest detective. It can not be a matter of scandal, for, a thousand pardons Wells, but he is not yet of the stature to incur scandal. A writer, a man of science, a man after much like yourself Watson, but less successful. It is not insult sir, but merely a recounting of facts as they stand today. In brief, the scandal free gentleman travels to see us, desperate, impoverished, with a case he fears he cannot afford and one he doubts we are able to solve. It must be a

7

matter of science, and from the newspaper coverage and my having read one of your earlier works over a rainy week end, I conclude the specific error being one of chronology, and the locked doors and the massive weight mentioned supported the possibility of a time device. Its absence implied that it had traveled in time and since we could ourselves not venture backward in time, our only path was to move forward in time, a path I may add we are forced to follow in any case. It is to our benefit that the device did not stray far, and has, in a way, returned to its master like a repentant dog."

I said nothing, but my face showed by disbelief.
"I recognized Wells immediately as I saw him from the curtained window it was so fortuitous you opened. He was clearly the same man shown in that article in the arts column of the Times a few months ago. I was perusing that section in regards to the involvement of an opera singer with a government official at the time. It turned out to be a minor matter.
"A set of circumstances that one can hardly credit, if one were writing a work of fiction," Wells said.
Another man would have shrugged off the comment, but Holmes was not one for such simian movements.
"The subject of the article was described as a man of science and the future. I see Wells that you have lost weight in the intervening months, no doubt as a result of your dual efforts."
"The device is not here, but it was impossible to remove. It is a matter of logic that your carriage has therefore not left and is still present."
"Are you blind Holmes?" I exclaimed, exasperated, when suddenly, the air filled with static. I became concerned that I had indeed approached too closely some innocuous looking hazard. A bizarre gust arose, strange in that all the doors and windows of the carriage house were firmly closed.

I was startled, but I daresay Holmes was bemused, when a large brassy contraption appeared before our very eyes. As my birthday was the following day, I suspected an elaborate prank on the part of my friend. It must be a sort of magician's trick that one sees in Piccadilly.

"I must have set the controls by mistake yesterday," Wells said sheepishly. "I have a fix for that," he added.

"A time machine," Holmes said nonchalantly.

"A time machine?" I questioned, my voice less level. "Balderdash."

My reaction was the same that an aboriginal might have experienced an identical sense of unease if faced with a gleaming four slice toaster.

I recovered my composure.

"Just in time for my birthday."

"Your birthday is tomorrow."

Wells had stood quietly as we, or I, marveled.

"It has no wheels?" Holmes questioned, although it was obvious that the machine lacked them.

"I don't intend to leave London," Wells replied.

"A man after your own heart, eh Holmes?" I joked.

"Quite. Nevertheless, it must be moved. Consider it".

"Payment?" Wells asked, instantly regretting the word, as he had already judged correctly Holmes' character.

"An adventure?" Wells reposited, simultaneous with Holmes' answer to the initial question.

"An adventure."

"She would be a beast to move. The fault is the quantity of copper in the machine, along with silver, and a more than a few slivers of gold. I have poured precious metal, a few melted sovereigns included I must say, into this masterpiece like paint into a mural. Slotted machines in Monte Carlo are less expensive. But it works. That is the joy."

9

I felt that the arrival of the time machine had displaced my powers of observation, as I did not follow the rapidity of the conversation.

"May we return the day after tomorrow?" Holmes asked. He was busy measuring the size of the machine.

"Does it run on petrol?"

"No. It uses forces of the sun and the earth's..." Holmes cut him off.

"It is undoubtedly very interesting, but I have no need to know how it works, only that it works."

"Our work is done here, I think Watson."

Are you available the day after tomorrow, I'd like to discuss this case in more detail?" Holmes addressed Wells.

"In the interim, I will arrange and pay to have an undercarriage with wheels attached tomorrow. Wells, you as expert, will of course supervise and approve. I would hate to hurry too quickly and, in our haste, meet ourselves in an awkward encounter. In any case, we have our own arrangements to make.

Tomorrow is indeed Watson's birthday. It is an important event for the dear doctor, for this day a year hence old friend, I expect you to be positively ancient, as aged as Methuselah. Wells, if you are free tomorrow evening," glancing at the wheelless carriage then at Wells' footwear, please join us, for a work free dinner. I can promise you fare much more appealing than English sole.

CHAPTER THREE Departure 1894

A few days later, ensconced in our lodgings, Holmes announced, "We leave tomorrow. Pack for a few days, a week at most. Bring your revolver, and some extra cartridges, I should think. Pack lightly. What is nonessential is just that."

"Where are we going?"

"We are leaving London for some time in the country. Stratford upon Avon."

"You are serious in this quest?"

"Yes."

"But why Holmes?"

"To follow the evidence. I need more data than a single centuries old book. Wells' device is ready, the modifications have been completed. It will transported to Victoria by a team of horses, taken by train to Stratford and finally to our departure point."

"You truly expect to meet him?" I asked, an image of a carved stone in a Stratford church springing unbid into my mind.

"I admit to a degree of doubt, but a search without doubt is without taste."

I ignored the context of his statement, so fixed was I on determining whether the words were his own of those of another.

Holmes and I set out for the train station, where Wells was scheduled to meet us. I had left a short note of our departure for Mrs. Hudson. What does one write in such circumstances that would not read as ravings? The innocuous message scribbled, we had left 221b Baker Street, perhaps for the last time.

Wells was waiting for us at Victoria station, the cargo safely loaded. He sat in the train compartment, as excited an American tourist.

The trip was uneventful. There was delay in Stratford as the teamsters aided in the unloading of the tarp covered time machine and hitched it to a team of huge draft horses. We followed in a separate carriage.

Holmes had chosen as our departure point one both practical and ironic. The hired men along with their powerful beasts muscled the time machine under the shade of a huge oak tree that sat in the ancient cemetery that would serve as our beginning or end. The men were paid off handsomely and left hurriedly, no doubt content to spend their bonus at their local pub as they discussed the latest bizarre behavior of Londoners.

We removed the tarp from the machine and placed our belongings inside.

We discovered that space was more limited than our collective thoughts had anticipated, forcing each of us to leave behind items that would have been deemed essential by one or the other. For me the camera was abandoned with regret, but I've eyes and a blank journal.

"Holmes," I commented, "you have packed more than my fashionable aunt. She can outfit a safari or high tea, both simultaneously if occasion requires it."

"If it is adventure you seek, I can supply it. High tea is another matter, and there you must find your own solution. There is no tea, Indian or otherwise."

The contents of Holmes' trunk did and would continue to astound me.

"Holmes and Watson, flamboyant magicians", Wells exclaimed in a voice suitable for a carnival."

"It is a sole act," I demurred, nodding to the single, scuffed duffel that now accompanied me, holding both my clothing and my medical supplies.

"The medicines inside are the true magic," I added in recognition of their silent power.

"Opium?" Holmes asked and then answered as one who well knew its effect, "Surely not a cure, but a lesser pain."

"It is near the moment," Wells said solemnly.

"I would prefer that we were moving forward, but that will come soon again."

Holmes leaned over and spoke quietly to me.

"To know the future, as our talented inventor is set on accomplishing, well, I will not criticize another's man quest, however incomprehensible is strikes me."

Wells remained silent, standing patiently as if a man with all the time in the world. The three of hoped, to varying degrees, that this was indeed the case.

We are to be on our way, and I press into the rough bark of the silent oak a quick note of our departure in case we never return.

We mounted the machine, my own sensation somewhere between ascending a scaffold and entering the main exhibit hall of a world fair. It was as stomach churning and intoxicating as my first day in Afghanistan. My old injury twinged as I found my seated between my two companions, our limited belongings stuffed into any open space. The arrangement, once determined, would serve us for the remainder of our sorties. I was reminded of a crowded channel crossing on one Holmes' and my less interesting cases, the Missing Bouton.

We were dressed in our 'costumes', period clothing that should permit us to blend in as merchants or even as a doctor. Holmes had rejected my suggestion to accent himself as a prelate, for religion is touchy in many eras.

"It is a marvelous creation," Wells proclaimed proudly. "It requires a team of strong horses to move hither and yon, but leaps centuries with the slight pressure of a single human finger."

"How does it work?" I asked.

"The universe consists of incalculable days and counts them like seconds as one uses a calendar to plan a dinner or to recall an anniversary. Sunrises and sunsets are but beads in a mechanical abacus, vastly improved of course. And then...".

Holmes was impatient.

"There will be time enough for explanations scientific. Let us away!"

Wells took control of our tiny ship, pushing rearward on a knobbed, brass lever. Light vanished, the only illumination a single dial in front of Wells. After what was the briefest moment and having felt the most miniscule movement, our pilot said quietly, without any sense of historic import, "Here we are," as daylight returned.

"That was quicker than I would have thought," remarked Holmes.

Wells laughed.

"We have only regressed a day."

"A trial then?"

"Yes. Hold on gentlemen," Wells advised and once again drew rearward on the brass lever that controlled our shared destinies.

We watched intently as the number rolled backward, the number of days increased, while the corresponding date indicator, geared with the day counter, showed yesterdates.

Days, week, years rolled by, there is no need to recount further for my readers the units of chronology.

By we, I mean to exclude Holmes from those fascinated by the dial, for a quick glance at our companion showed by the dim glow that his eyes were closed, his head leaned back. It was the same unperturbable pose I'd seen on the train ride from London.

I thought of our lodgings in Baker street; would we ever seem them again, or would my last, brief missive left behind be the last clue of Holmes and Watson? Would we have left a trail that no detective on earth could follow? And

Wells too, I added silently. Was this a fatal whim, one driven by Holmes' ennui and cocaine, to which I had succumbed, or were myself and Wells equally culpable, pushed by our own desires and curiosity?

My focus shifted to the cramped rear. Our luggage nestled as oblivious as Holmes. Would I have need of the medicine and instruments therein? An image of the horrors of Afghanistan sprang to mind and I wished that I had been able to pack more supplies.

I must pause here a moment to describe our transit. As with the one day trial of only a moment or centuries earlier, or should I say later, there was no sense of movement, no swaying of the carriage. The ride would not have garnered a farthing at a fair in Brighton. It was sedate, boring as Holmes' snoring confirmed.

It was a flutter of blackness of light and darkness, each so brief that it brought on nausea. Wells peered at the dial, through a tunnel he made with his hands, his nose nearly touching the glass that covered the counter.

We finally stopped, the sun was setting, and we were alive. The surrounding atmosphere was fresh with the scent of ferns, crushed under our taxi, filling our nostrils.

We had begun the voyage under the shade of a tree, centuries old. The area was level and had made for an excellent launching block, isolated as it was from darting eyes. The tree was now thinner but no less magnificent, evidence of our movement in time.

I am perhaps now an expert on the phenomena, but at the moment following our first trip in Time, it was troubling in a near indescribable fashion, to see the dead disappear, to regain flesh and blood and assume their temporary roles among the living. A few fresh graves for stale bodies, and legible markers stood where had once been hundreds. I heard, or imagined, the bells of a distant cathedral.

Starlit and moonless, we had arrived on a less than holy night for our search for witches, betrayal, and horrific murder. Dawn was only a few breaths away. A long walk to 1611 lay before us.

CHAPTER FOUR Shakespearean Stratford

"The pound note is worth nothing here, whereas Nature's creations endure, fire, air," Holmes paused then added, " gold.". He then distributed to us old coinage, in both silver and gold. As I accepted the money, I thought of Chaucer's Pardoner's Tale. We were three also, searching for Death.

"Where did you obtain these?" asked Wells, as yet unfamiliar with Holmes' methods.

"I was given these by one of the curators of the British Museum. My brother Mycroft was of some assistance, as these," Holmes said, jingling a few pieces in his hand, "are not a loan. It is a reverse bestowal, although it is within the realm of possibility that we will return them to their original owners."

We chanced upon three women doing laundry who kindly directed us to the public house where we would certainly find Master Shakespeare.

When they thought we were beyond earshot I heard them mocking and laughing at our odd attire.

She was a classic English beauty sentenced by chance to labor in a destitute century, serving cretins, her only unrealized joy being to rub elbows with the Bard. That acquaintance would not feather her bed, and she was likely to die of a young age in childbirth or infection from diseased teeth.

17

Wells must have read my depressing thoughts as we sat in the pub, for he said, "The world is not fair, doctor."

"I pray that it improves," I replied.

"Prayers have been tried enough to prove their futility. It is politics and people, aided by technology that will improve our state. That has been demonstrated beyond refute. It is only the pace that needs to be accelerated."

"Optimism drives you?" I asked.

"I am English, with one foot in Heaven and the other in...".

"Hell?"

"Mud," Wells replied with a chuckle, for indeed he had one foot in the muck that covered large portions of the floor.

"I am irritated at myself, and with Holmes."

"And with me?"

Wells shrugged, a motion that cut me deeply. I was accustomed to Holmes' gauche attempts at compliment, but to be judged a cypher by a dreamer was offensive.

"I apologize sincerely," Wells said quickly. The man was as attentive to emotion and bodily nuance, or lack thereof, of his interlocuter as Holmes was to facts and the testimony of inanimate objects.

I comforted my ego with the realization that we were physicians three, each with our own specialty. Three doctors, and a trio of witches, were we all that different?

Upon landing, for that was how I thought of our magical flight through time, we had argued.

"We should mount guard if we are to risk being stranded here," Holmes had suggested.

"Given that you have little interest in the past, it is reasonable to ask you to stay behind."

Wells was adamant that the device was inoperable without him and that if either of us wanted sole guard duty or if Holmes and I wanted to split the responsibility between the two of us of nannying a machine, that was fine by him, but he was unwilling to miss a living history lesson. Moreover, we were only three in number in a foreign land and there was safety in numbers.

Holmes and I relented, for we could refute neither his logic nor the temptation he described.

We were here on a mission, however Quixotic it might seem in hindsight, being cavaliere did not include extended periods of nursemaiding a futuristic horseless carriage.

Yet no sooner had we reached the center of Stratford, than Holmes disappeared, promising to return within an hour, two at the most. I was accustomed to Holmes' unexplained absences, but it was new to Wells.

As we sat in the pub, awaiting our expedition leader, Wells commented, "I understand Holmes. He is single minded when he is on a case, as I am with my machine, and as your undoubtedly are Doctor with your patients."

I nodded in agreement.

Holmes was already at work. My friend was the best evidence of divine gift while being among its most scoffing detractor. It was David denying the existence of Michelangelo. Good and evil were so real to him yet strictly confined to the non-supernatural.

The hunt or game as Holmes called, was afoot, and Holmes was always magnificently human in those moments. It was his private joie de vivre. What separates passion from addiction, I wondered.

One can excel at either, or both I admitted sadly. Is it a life if one fails or succeeds at either? Or both?

A shadow fell across the table, and I looked up to find my friend standing there.

"What is the house selection?" Holmes asked as if we found ourselves in a new club in Belgravia.

"Beer is the safest beverage available. I have iodine tablets for water."

19

"Or for the ale," Wells quipped.

"Rainwater is an option also. I spied a barrel as I entered."

"It is indeed a wonder that humanity has survived such conditions, only to progress to the slums of modern London," Wells commented sarcastically.

"Your cup is half empty, Holmes observed with a downward glance.

"Nearly empty," Wells responded, then completely vacated it with a backward tilt of his head.

"How do you measure yours Watson?"

"Nary a drop."

Holmes left to bring fresh drinks and returned with a fourth to fill the empty chair around our table.

He was a man of about 50 years of age, with clean clothes and fingernails, a man of sufficient means to not labor. He was courteous to us as he was to others in the pub, those who labored treated as princely as ourselves. I wondered if this man was himself the man we sought.

He had introduced himself as Roger Cardenio, but he carried no trace of the Spaniard in his features. His accent was unplaceable.

Eventually we maneuvered the conversation to the subject of Shakespeare.

"He is our best-known resident, a great success that reflects well on this village. A curse to be in first place, for from the pinnacle there is but descent.

"Have you read his work?"

The man looked a bit askance at the question. "Have I seen his plays? I have."

He looked again at us curiously. He echoed my question back to me.

"Have you read his work?"

"Indeed, I have. For who has not...".

Holmes interrupted.

"Who has not seen his plays has not attended theatre."

"His plays are theatre," Wells added unnecessarily.

"Quite," I said, feeling myself a buffoon in an ad-hoc farce.

Cardenio regarded us each in turn, judging our level of soberness. He found it adequate, for he continued our conversation.

"Master Shakespeare has progressed recently from men who think themselves gods, to gods who behave as cretins. He is a keen observer of both men and gods, I think."

"And witches," Holmes interjected, but the lure sank, ignored.

"It is a pity that both he and I chant from the sanctity of temple of Bacchus, where all powerful villains are easily drowned."

"He comes here?" I asked

"Yes."

"Stratford is indeed blessed to have two great wits, sir. And we find ourselves only newly arrived. Are there others?"

"This is a normal English village, gentlemen. There are great wits and those who are halfway along."

"Yet even two is uncommon."

"Two is not odd, I think."

Holmes smiled faintly at the repartee. Cambridge has nothing over an English pub I can proclaim confidently.

"Is it the water, the air, the bucolic environment that accounts for this marvel?"

It was Cardenio's turn to smile.

"A distant cousin?" Holmes asked.

"Not so distant, but recently close," was the enigmatic response.

"I am by halves pilgrim and tourist," commented Stratford's second resident poet.

"Shakespeare's stage is the world, I limit myself to this hall for I am a drunk," Cardenio said soberly.

"One would not notice," Holmes observed.

"Your eyes are clear, and your voice is steady. You are an actor as well as a philosopher."

"One cannot be one without the other. One must remain one. As to sobriety, one can be drunk from vapors of boastfulness and fear. It is a witches' brew. Such drunkenness giveth the performance but taketh away the desire."

I raised my eyebrows in surprise.

"You say afraid?"

"What wise man is not? What wise man does not keep fear on retainer? I have seen sights that...but I shall not dwell on future horrors. They are mythical until tomorrow manifests itself over yonder hill," Cardenio said, pointing to a wall, beyond which lay presumably higher ground to the east.

"Here is serenity, where one hears news from the outside, from other travelers such as yourselves. Although none so recently as tantalizing as yourselves. No matter, I will not pry, for this is refuge for all, tourists and pilgrims included. Stories are carried in through that door," and again he pointed, providing useless stage directions to his small audience.

"These stories are muddied from their long voyage, yet when they are delivered, I find them digestible plates of edible mush. The world has survived the period between action yonder and reception hither. Time provides a wonderful escape.

Travelers recount between these walls their harrowing catastrophes, their explosive talk like the crash of a musket in the forest. The deafening sound does not echo, and its momentary novelty is forgotten as the birds recommence their song. Tweet, tweet" he added as illustration.

"Even drunks must depart sometime, and I find now my exit. I bid farewell, dear gentlemen."

He shook our hands, turned and left, as steady on his feet as any man ever was.

Wells commented first.

"The drinks here must be weakly served. For tourist and pilgrims, no doubt."

"We will see for ourselves," I replied.

"We will need lodgings as well," Holmes added, defining the night's mission for we three pilgrims and tourists.

The following morning, we inquired of the innkeeper if Master Shakespeare was in town.

His wife and family, aye, but he himself is not expected until tomorrow. His comings and goings are his own of course, but he has habits like any man.

"We will tour the town," Wells said to us without enthusiasm.

"He will return tomorrow," I countered. "We can advance a day."

"We will make no more trips than necessary," Wells commanded. "We will tour the tour. And we did."

1611 Stratford upon Avon was not two days large.

A repast of broiled eels and well boiled vegetables provided a hearty meal for our self guided tour. The village we recognized in parts, other, due to their age, were new to our eyes. The prime example of this reversed state of affairs was of course Shakespeare's splendid house which stood testimony to his presence and success.

I cursed for the first time my loss at not having brought a camera along with us. I consoled myself with the knowledge that had I been able to take photographs, they would have been as universally judged false, as contrived and unconvincing as if I had presented photographic evidence of dinosaurs alive in South America.

Instead, I committed to memory aide by my own crude drawings of each marvel. Such carbon representations were subsequently used by a discrete artist, formerly of the Strand, to create illustrations that I retain as cherished memories.

We passed our evenings at the pub. We did not see Cardenio again, nor was the barmaid from the first night to be found serving customers.

"Has she died already?" I asked aloud, my tone sad, for without them, the evening would pass slowly.

"She was healthy and lacked the post-partum sagging buttocks," I commented.

"Stillbirth, starvation, childhood accident, death is a frequent visitor to this village, if not a semi-resident," Wells said. "It is a time that oscillates between bucolic and bubonic. This is a criminal beyond your reach Holmes," he said quietly, his sorrow evident at being the bearer of bad news.

"Watson here has treated women in childbirth. You have saved and you have lost. Is that not true?"

I nodded.

"It is a tragic event, not made less so by its lack of rarity. There are limits to life's preciousness. I accept the dispassionate hand of Death and his diseases, Wells," Holmes responded equally somberly.

"The past and future are equally abhorrent. I choose to be a man of his time. The present is inescapable here in the past as what you might term elsewhen."

"You are a pessimist Holmes," Wells exclaimed with paradoxical delight in his voice.

"The world follows a diurnal cycle, and boredom follows adventure as day follows night. The days grow shorter, peace or war and the former I do not find peaceful. Watson, what say you?"

"War infects a man, and he either vomits it or acquires a hunger for it that must be fed periodically."

"There must be no war," Wells protested.

There we left it momentarily;, an armistice on war. It saddened each of us, I'm sure for we realized that we were all a bit wrong.

"Did you mean what you said?" I asked Holmes.

"About war?"

"Yes."

"You are the wordsmith, Watson. Soften war into violence, conflict, dispute, if you choose to commit this adventure to ink. No one shall believe a word of it. As to human nature, it speaks for itself."

A moment later, he passed judgement.

"Conflict I think will slide neatly into your narrative."

The 17th century pub, like its modern counterpart was a center for gossip and preening. It was the natural habitat of actors.

A loud, clear voice reached out table.

"The witches are central to the play."

Was it Shakespeare himself? No only an actor seated with others at a distant table.

"Three witches. If a man be a devil, what is his rib? Less, or more? Satan has lock stopped us beyond the gate; our most faithful and feckless companion."

"He's good inn't he, one of the locals praised him, nudging Wells who appeared in need of encouragement.

"We three are bound and branded. Three is more magic than two, dangerously stable."

"Witches?" Holmes asked the local, a hint of ridicule in his voice.

"Oh, they're about," the hanger-on corroborated.

The actor spoke, this time his words seemed his own.

"Witches are beauty, among us the most elegant, disguised, and quality grist, for Master Shakespeare's mill. As am I, and all that walk or fly o'er this land."

And with that the actor bowed and sat down again to polite applause.

"This island is a nation of hardy poets," Holmes said to Wells to me.

"Ireland lies to the west, Holmes," I argued.

Wells said, "We are fortunate interlopers. We don't belong here, not as these locals who surround us. They are tocals."

"Time locals," he added for clarification.

"Very pithy," Holmes admitted.

"As to these tocals, it is not their presence but their odor that impinges on my desire to remain here. Really gentlemen, one can enjoy only for so long the wonders of London Zoo on a stifling summer day, despite the marvels within its grounds. Shakespeare inhabits the past, you pair the tempestuous present, me I am destined for the future.

"All times equally squalid I would wager but my winning would bring neither of us joy," responded Holmes..

I offered my perspective.

"What a horror to be marooned here, Crusoes without hope, life sentences in a foreign, escape proof prison."

Wells nodded agreement.

"Gas light, clean sheets, sanitary restaurants, water closets, all to be invented. This is as primitive as Afghanistan. They are family but I feel that we are not the same tribe. Generational differences were never more stark. As for you Wells, I wonder what you will find tomorrow in the future."

"To know the past is boring comfort, a conceited satisfaction that today is wiser. I can only imagine that seeing tomorrow's tomorrow would constitute a graphic terror. Any ceramic vase of hope would be vaporized as if struck by

26

a locomotive. Tomorrow is our offspring, for the childless as well. I pray it turns out better than I fear."

"That which exists can be altered," Wells countered. He continued.

"Their problems are not mine. Is it true only because they will muddle through and then they will die. I find is depressingly easy to discount their misery, for it is temporary.

It is nonexistent in the world, even here jolly England. It makes all of this, and all that is to come meaningless. Does it not?" He asked, searching for encouragement in the form of denial.

It was not offered.

None of us were simple enough to merit lies.

"It is only a game, whispered Holmes. One plays well and therein lies contentment, for a while."

"Contentment is for the cemetery," Wells volunteered.

"You believe the dead to be content?" I asked.

"Assuredly not. The dead are dead. The birds and squirrels which there reside are content of no human contact, the rare visitor aside. Let the dead bury the dead and then let them all rest in peace. The future is bright, the present and past, why that is much of a muchness.

"Is it?" Holmes questioned. "Does it trouble you Watson, as it does me, that we three lose sight of our track, and grow nostalgic and sentimental?

Wells, you are the expert. Is this melancholy I perceive and find weakening my faculties a form of temporal seasickness?"

Wells reflected and Holmes consulted me for a second opinion.

"Watson, you are the medical man. What say you?"

Like Wells, I too pondered without reply.

An impatient Holmes offered his own diagnosis.

"Too much fresh air and the lack of noise frees the mind to focus on and then dwell upon inconsequentialities. Give it no more thought. It is stimulus and response. Lacking the one, one atrophies.

Oh but this town is dishearteningly quiet. It is no wonder that Shakespeare is successfully at staging violence and intrigue, for he is selling water in the desert. Little matter that the water is tepid and brackish.

I shall be content to inhale the noxious fumes of modern London. I may write a monograph comparing and contrasting the sounds and scents of the various epochs. Regretfully, two data points are insufficient to draw valid conclusions."

If it was not unimaginable, I would have diagnosed my friend as suffering homesickness.

"My two nostrils beg to differ. Must I grow a third? I detect putridity with my current pair," Wells joked.

"News travels at the speed of Cardenio's infrequent visitors. There are no personal columns, there are no newspapers. There is no panoply of data. There is nothing...".

Newspapers; the wonder and bane of modern life. For Holmes and I to a much lesser degree, the twice dailies were as a satisfying as a needle, a nip, or a pipe. More compelling for Holmes than cocaine, as the drug was an escape when the daily journals lacked sufficient stimulus.

Here there was neither. Cocaine was as unobtainable as the Times. Even our tobacco was limited, although Holmes seemed to pay this shortage no mind and smoked regularly. 1611 was raw and primitive, in scene as well as in deed. I must confess that such uncertainty and hardship was irresistible.

"It is not an insurmountable challenge," Wells responded to Holmes' complaint.

"I propose...".

Whatever was to follow I cannot say, for Holmes rejected Wells' premise unheard.

"Only death remains insurmountable, and millions of faithful reject even that constraint. As for us, we will find a way. Time," and he paused to let settle upon us the power of the word, "is on our side. This is not a fair game and for that I am grateful to you Wells for being favored."

I interjected, as the conversation was achieving nothing.

"Holmes, it is your turn."

Holmes stood and headed to the bar.

"Are witches real?" asked Wells, his query launched as a momentary lull struck the hubbub of the pub. One man guffawed, while another man, stooped and elderly, scurried toward the door. Their actions were I am sure, mere coincidence, not response.

The actor rose to the occasion.

"If you can imagine it, whom am I to deny its existence? I cannot see inside your mind, try I might. I have heard that evil comes in threes, be they deaths, witches, or strangers to Stratford.

"Master?" Wells prompted for clarification, and the actor, disconcerted by the unmerited sobriquet, deflected.

"There is but one master," declining to identify such personage. "Do you believe they exist, sir?"

"No," Wells replied firmly.

"And you?" asked the actor in a stage voice that carried to the ears of the publican.

"Assuredly," replied the robust man, adding with impeccable timing, "Master."

The guffawer exploded on cue. When the echoes of laughter subsided, the audience receptive for more of this repartee, the thespians delivered.

"You are both correct, for verily there is only truth on tap in taverns. As far as today's truth, I think it fitting that our witch denying new friend pay the drinks and our broom flying publican pour them."

It was a decision worthy of a sober Solomon, and there nearly ended the scene.

Another voice, one that I would soon recognize as Shakespeare's, opined "Their sex renders them as evil as our desire for them transforms us." It is strange now to realize he was at times a man of few words for one of so many. One must learn to listen before one may speak.

I craved to conduct a proper interview, one with copious notes, for posterity will curse me when they read that I passed on such an opportunity. I beg their future indulgence in not finding these golden scraps brass.

CHAPTER FIVE Shakespeare

How shall I describe Shakespeare? Now, here after having met and spoken with him, I state succinctly, he was anti-Holmes. I reflected long before writing the afore few words. Many readers will recall the arch-criminal Moriarty whose was the anti-Holmes. The evil to the good.

Shakespeare was kind, generous, no trace of evil seen or experienced. But he was emotional, energetic to the point of having excised the concept of lethargy and melancholy when one was in his presence. In this way he was anti-Holmes.

He did not interrupt, he did not preempt, and yet in his own slovenly dressed manner (I was most surprised at his casual dress), he bordered as a mirror of my friend. It was their eyes that disclosed them as distant twins. Orbs are paired windows of the soul either could have said, for this shared trait they recognized equally.

I reached the above conclusion after having sat with, drank with, and spoken with the man.

Holmes made the first move in establishing contact with our 'witness'.

Seated at our table, he reached into a pocket and withdrew a package wrapped in elegant paper and passing it to the barmaid, whom Holmes referred to her name, Darles, asked that it be delivered to Shakespeare with our compliments.

The package thus sent as emissary, Holmes continued to speak to us of nothing special, for the life of me I cannot recall the subject.

A moment later, Darles returned with an invitation from Shakespeare to join us at his table, the largest by far in the pub.

"Sit gentlemen," Shakespeare said in a full, pleasant voice.

The package sat unopened on the table before its recipient.

"To what do I owe a gift from three strangers? It is not Midwinter and I am not an infant in straw."

"We wish to meet and speak with Master Shakespeare," Holme said simply.

"We are met, and we are speaking. A gift is not necessary."

"But welcome, I hope?" Wells asked.

"Of course. Gifts are welcome, hope included. The paper is exquisite, I must confess I have never spied its equal, and itself comprises a gift. But let us see the inside. It is enjoyable I think you magi to be present at the unswaddling."

With that Shakespeare carefully opened the package, spreading the paper to its full extent. There inside sat a pair of gloves, at first glance it was clear they were appropriately sized. They were magnificent, the highest quality, peccary hide from South America, known as the world's best, yet heretofore unseen in England.

Shakespeare picked them up from the table, and after a moment of regarding closely the workmanship, slid his hands into the supple leather hand coverings.

"They are as you say, more appropriate for Midwinter," Holmes stated.

"Incredible gentlemen. These are otherworldly. My father, were he alive, would remark the craftsman."

After a long moment he removed the gloves, placed them carefully on top of the paper which he in turn folded.

"What it is you wish to discuss?" Then as Holmes pulled his pipe from a breast pocket, Shakespeare stopped him with a hand gesture.

"His majesty King James judges tobacco bad for the lungs and who am I to dispute a man both blessed by the Good Lord and with the best doctors in the known world."

Holmes must have sensed my medical discomfort at the unintended slight, for he smiled as he returned his pipe to its place.

"We saw your Scottish play quite recently," I said.

Shakespeare appeared confused.

"Macbeth?" Shakespeare queried after a moment. "My Scottish play, what an unusual turn of phrase."

"It had the ring of truth to it," I said, completing the two lines I had been issued by my own playwright to utter. The scene thus set; I fell silent.

"Yet something seems amiss," ventured Holmes.

"I am familiar with history and truth."

"Have you gold as well?" Shakespeare asked with a smile.

Shakespeare's eyes were fixed on Holmes', like a constable regarding a miscreant apprehended in the act. He listened attentively, expectantly, ready to commit each word to eternal memory for use at a later date, in another setting.

Holmes faltered, hesitant to criticize the achievement of a legend, alive and not long time dead and therefore insensitive to insult.

"A Chinaman was at market last week, with abacus and gold. I say Chinaman, for he dressed the part, but otherwise was as bizarre and normal as you three. I myself have no experience with men from the East.

He could have been Russian or from one of the lost tribes. Abacus and gold, the chains of a self-sentenced prisoner. Life is less than poetry yet more than abaci. And the past."

Wells spoke.

"The past is dust that either puts me to sleep or makes me sneeze. The future, well, now that is a different animal."

"It is an undiscovered country. I'm disappointed in the future as I won't be there to criticize it. As to my current criticism, how many stories remain, not all dregs. My harshest critics are here," his magnificent writing hand, then flesh, made an idle gesture towards the pub's thirsty, "and I have as defense only plume and parchment. But I adore it."

"Fame?" I prompted.

"Is a short, wicked flame. It is as sonorous as boos, as brief as applause."

"What then?" queried Holmes.

"Creation fills the day more fully that draughts," he stated, our eyes following his as they shifted to the pair in game across the room.

"Searching for marital and familial advice in a tavern is a poor first choice. But for drama there is no better vantage point. My unpaid actors lodge here, they write their own lines and angers. I merely enhance and magnify. With my loupe I see craters where others observe glowing beauty."
"

Holmes had his own game of draughts to see to completion. He had told me once that well rounded people are smooth pebbles in a stream. It is the sharp edge flint that leaves impression.

Holmes proceeded, undeterred.

"Is MacBeth accurate history?"

"History is yesterday's present and future entangled in human recall."

In the silence that followed, Shakespeare saw that Holmes craved an improved answer.

The Elizabethan sighed. It sorrowed me that one day his last breath would occur thusly. I interpreted his sigh as disappointment that his interlocutor was unable to appreciate the response and required more lucidity.

"I see that a pithy pun will not sate the hunger of my new odd friend who is a stranger to the fare at my table and finds it indigestible yet sits with a greater appetite than my local inquisitors.

Gossip is uncured history. The pride relishes raw meat. I think you different, you seek to calm your animal spirit."

Holmes smiled. "You feed the multitude. I applaud you."

Wells added his voice, "A man must be naïve to believe in something, but a fool to believe in nothing."

"What man is not both?" Shakespeare answered.

"The actors change, the play remains. Which plays well is the choice well made. There is little gold in unvarnished truth, for it shines too brightly to attract the eye."

Shakespeare looked at the gift before him.

"Do the gloves therein remain? If I think it, they do."

He did not touch the package.

"The Scottish play. Odd. But then three is odd, your team doubly so. Cardenio has thriced himself.

This one," he said indicating Holmes, "perfect for someone not deserving a part in any play I could write. His height would grant him a role as backdrop, yet he lacks breadth for a convincing curtain. No, he's best in the stands, where his towering would be to his benefit.

The second," a slight gesture directed in my direction, "content to remain here with wine, women, and wrestling, and the third, the young traveler, anxious to be anywhere but where he tardies at present."

Shakespeare drank from his cup.

"You say that you saw the Scottish play some yesterday. The ink on that play is dry a good six years. Five years elapsed between the royal and second performance. That history is accurate.

Can either of us vouch for events from five centuries ago?"

If the comment had been directed solely to me, I fear that the mild rebuke would have been as forever painful as my Afghan wound.

Holmes was nonplussed and sat his turn as expectantly as Shakespeare had sat his.

I wondered then if Shakespeare tolerated such questions only as a means of being later to jail strangers in ink and paper. There was, one might say, method to his courtesy."

"You demand my history of another history, when for the past five years I have been living and writing in more distant pasts. It all begins to blur. We are much of the same age, the age of retire. You send questions perfectly gloved, but my responses are delivered by gnarled hands. Inside those pig skin gauntlets, my hands are obscured and styled elegant.

All we know is false. True for an hour, and then inedible as week old bread. While fresh we feed upon it greedily and spurn it later, repulsed.

My own words fade as if I talk to the wind.

History is a sequence of day and night, my learned acquaintance and if one were to ask us, 'T'is light or night?'"

He paused, awaiting a response.

"T's evening twilight" Holmes replied.

"Well done," Shakespeare exclaimed.

I felt myself in Heaven. If I live to be one hundred, I will never forget the pride I felt in Holmes that hour, nor the amusement at the only blush I witnessed spread across his cheeks.

"An excellent student deserves reward," Shakespeare commented. "One made perfect with another round."

"An excellent teacher merits the thanks of his student," Holmes responded as he stood to order the round. Before he turned completely from the table, I do believe I saw a smile cross his face. But I cannot be sure, for indeed, it was twilight.

CHAPTER SIX We must go further back

The next morning after our encounter with Shakespeare, Holmes was still quiet. While I had been ecstatic and Wells was content to return to his true passion, the future, Holmes said barely a word as we shared a simple breakfast. Sustenance consumed, we huddled and discussed what our own future would entail.

Holmes began.

"I do not intend to criticize the poet. He is a master weaver of words, and conjurer of entertaining dreams that can be shared by the hordes. Its better than bear baiting, and less bloody. Shakespeare knows much but not the much we seek. He is but a messenger, the greatest of heralds notwithstanding He knows it all and forgotten half. To our benefit it was the wrong half. For if he had enforced his testimony, this travel would have been in vain. As I said in Baker Street Watson, he is a poet, not an historian."

Wells and I were silent, awaiting the conclusion of his soliloquy.

"We must go further back, to 1041."

We looked around at what would be our last view of 1611, whichever way the coin landed.

"We will advance to our time and then travel by train to London, and then on to Scotland, and then..."

Wells interrupted.

"I agree that we return to our time, but there we stop. The farther one ventures afield, spatially or temporally, I theorize that errors increase, compounding at an increasing rate."

"You speak of your machine?" Holmes questioned

Wells nodded.

"My machine is not a hansom cab but a delicate precision instrument The more we use my invention, the more obvious become its limitations."

"Such as what?" I queried.

"We have made but a few trips," Holmes said.

"I have not enough time to explain, Doctor," Wells stated his concern without irony. "We should return to the world before we are marooned here."

Holmes reached into his pocket for tobacco but reconsidered and sat motionless for a moment.

"The world," Holmes said, bemused it seemed at the idea of being marooned in Britain.

"Knowing what the future brings is as fearsome as ignorance of tomorrow's events."

"Which means what?" I asked

"You agree with me?" Wells asked, relieved.

"I agree that we return to the world as you so appealingly describe it. Once there, you may perform any necessary repairs or maintenance as you see fit."

Seeing the direction in which Holmes was heading Wells began to protest.

Holmes raised a hand as a request to be heard.

"The machine will need the work done if you are to make your trip into the future. I will finance the repairs, and any that are needed upon our return from 1041."

Wells considered the alternative, and nodded agreement.

"With your support, I can have the work done within a few hours. If we remain here, it will require two centuries."

"It is settled then," I said.

CHAPTER SEVEN 1041

We returned to present day Stratford, then by train, we reached Scotland. Finally, by horsedrawn carriage to our launch point. Unsure how long we would be in 1041, we advantaged ourselves of modernity and took a supply of baths in advance.

The darker Scotland became as we retreated into the past the more Heavenly grew the night sky. Coal gas and electricity illumination extinguished into tomorrow and candles in their turn became rare.

Wells spoke as we traveled backward in time.

"I did not anticipate making so many trips. I've mentioned before that this is a prototype. This past is past poisonous," he said as way of regretting his decision to embark on this voyage, which I know realize possessed qualities of a folly.

The change from one century to another was stepping outside from a Swiss greenhouse to wintry alpine valley in the shadow of the Matterhorn. The world was differently the same. Two entirely different worlds occupying the same space.

I have no evidence to present the reader of this trip, for our compartment was as crowded as before. Other than the words themselves that I have recorded to the best of my recollection, my hands are empty. This is not my first adventure with Holmes, but certainly the earliest.

I broke from my reverie to ask a question of Wells.

"How can you be certain of the date?"

"The sun is never late in its orbit around us," he explained. I could not prevent a quick glance at Holmes, who smirked in appreciation of another human who joined him in astro-ignorance

"It remains to the machine to simply count, accounting for leap days along the way. It is absolute value whether forward or back in time. Elementary, gentlemen."

"Elementary," confirmed Holmes.

I feel that a description of our conveyance will benefit the particularly curious reader.

It was cramped but with excessive headroom. Wells claimed it was a safety precaution as it provided additional space for breathable air. We were as three adults stuffed into a child's carousel carriage where we remained stationary as the world, in utter darkness, whirled by silently. A few notes of flute music and the bizarre image would have been complete.

We exchanged few words and I suspect that if we have traveled more slowly the oxygen in our bubble would have been consumed to the point of our asphyxiation. On the contrary, we traveled quickly, the journey taking less time by our measure than a hansom from Baker street to Piccadilly. We had traveled more than eight centuries without having advanced an inch.

If Wells had not relented on the control lever, we might have arrived at the beginning, a blackless, borderless starlight. We stopped, and daylight filled the time machine's compartment.

An eagle climbed above us and then swooped down near us, as it debated between attack and retreat at our sudden appearance. Air, stirred by the beast's great wings, brought to our sensitive nostrils the stench of death. A days old stag lay nearby in tall, harsh grass, a scant ten paces distant from our time cab.

"Two deaths upon arrival does not an auspicious beginning make," Holmes commented.

I looked again at the death scene and noticed that it was indeed a pair of magnificent antlered creatures that had locked horns, only to find undignified death in the desolate landscape.

"This pair, alive and without our anachronistic presence would have been worthy of Constable," I remarked.

We covered the machine, put on cloaks and muddied our fine footwear, my boots more costly than my wife would have enjoyed hearing. Mary was forward in the world as we considered the future, and yet when I returned to that world, I would be a three year widower. While real, the past was dreamlike, a combination that could prove dangerous, if not fatal. We were more than mere observers to a museum. Here the exhibits could bite, and stab.

"These are terrible times," I said.

Neither of my companions disagreed.

Localized as best we could, in mud and not forest greens, we began our march to the castle of Macbeth a mile or more to the east, I reckoned.

The flesh of the dead stags would soon disappear leaving only bones beside our return vehicle which sat disguised next to a huge, cold, rugged boulder, an item which Providence had seen fit to gift Scotland in abundance.

As we reversed time, as I have previously noticed, the night sky of the past became clearer, as the smokey press of human activity receded into the future. I cannot comment on whether it was a fair trade, and I can only leave further thought on the clash between man and Nature to that day that finds us once again safe in Baker Street.

It was odd to be homesick within near eyesight of one's home, or where one's birthplace would one day sprout. But homesick I was. By Wells' reckoning we were in Scotland on Saturday, July 4, 1041.

In a France that was scarcely a step away compared to our own modern world William was not yet a legend. Was that not more pressing than the death of minor king in Scotland? What was happening across the channel today?

According to Wells, our present lay along a similar channel, a nebulous one-sided corridor, which each room a distinct habitation for a registered moment.

"Time slips away since we leave it unleashed.

Would you expect it to sit attentively like a trained guide dog/hound?"

I'm not sure I understood a word of what he said.

Was today a counterfeit moment, ourselves uninvited guests in another's suite.

I cannot say. I only remember that it was warm in Scotland on July 4, 1041.

Hastings was history, far less important than crime, I knew to Holmes.

Did Wells speak French, I wondered. Little matter for today predates the Norman conquest. French won't benefit us. English may destroy us.

"Watson?" One word and I felt myself back in primary school, braced before the instructor, himself indistinguishable from others of his species.

43

Good teachers are as replaceable as a soldier in an excellent regiment.

"How is your Gaelic?"

"Gaelic? I can try."

"This may help," Holmes said, passing me a new but incongruously dog eared Gaelic-English lesson book

The words and intonations returned to me in a rush and my temporary flashback to childhood evaporated like a stoker's sweat on a glowing boiler.

I nodded my acceptance.

"That is the spirit.'

Once committed I did my duty. During our time in 1041, I spoke like a child to men half my age and they accepted me as either a dimwit or a foreigner, interchangeable judgments in their eyes. It was normal behavior yet it shamed me to think that I behaved similarly and would likely do so again when we returned to our time. I vowed to minimize the action of which I was now the recipient.

I looked at my watch as I pulled it from my 11th century costume. It was time to meet the MacBeth of history.

We soon found a path which led to what passed for a road.

It was a beautiful day, but as I have already said, terrible times. As we passed into a heavily shaded section of the dirt road, we were attacked by a band of robbers, three or four in number, I cannot be sure of the number as in any combat, it occurred at a pace that was both incredibly slow and blindingly past. Wells and I quickly defended ourselves from our attackers and they disappeared into the shadowy undergrowth.

Holmes rapid movement disarmed the slightly built man. I could not push from my mind the fear that this dazed Scotsman sprawled in the dust, should come to fatal harm. Would such a death result in my own extinguishment. I was tempted to unload then and there my service revolver and consign it to non-use. My scientific mind quickly rejected the idea as statistically incredibly improbable. If perchance I relied on faulty probabilities, I was unlikely to notice my own disappearance.

I was on the verge of explaining my thought process to Holmes but forsook that step in seeing him extend a hand to the flattened man and lifting him to his feet.

"A cousin of yours, Watson?" he asked sardonically.

"One can avoid the odor by positioning oneself upwind of Watson's ancestors," Holmes quipped.

"In our own London it is the city itself and not its rugged inhabitants that perfume poorly the air."

Holmes was normally a quick study yet I, who had seen him in action on innumerable occasions, was amazed by the acuity by which he progressed in the unfamiliar language.

Our assailant turned guide, informed us that we were indeed close to the castle, which lay over the next ridge. He indicated that we were not the first group he had greeted in such a unique fashion but the sole to have defeated them. The man, Ian stated that his team must have been exhausted, accounting for the unexpected, for them, outcome.

To Ian's surprise, Holmes complimented them on their athleticism, but suggested that there was more profit in courtesy than in crime. To demonstrate his point, he offered a few small coins to the man in reward for his service as guide.

"We need no enemies, in your hometown Watson," he said as we continued on our way.

"It is dangerous times when every man may be king," Wells observed.

We expected to find a remote, bleak castle. Instead we were met with a fair.

We walked the commons gaily decorated and filled with the majority of inhabitants likely residing within a two hours walk.

It was a gorgeous day, with the sun seeming to linger over booths of interest.

We found a booth that served beverages and offered seating and a view of the festivities.

Before entering, Holmes warned us.

"A foreign tongue transforms us into conspirators. Conspiracies abound so suspicion is warranted. Singly, any of us would serve as harmless novelty for these Scotsmen."

Holmes switched to Gaelic, and I followed his lead, as Wells remained silent.

"Which language will our driver speak in the future?" Holmes asked rhetorically.

"I hope he finds a future where English is still spoken."

Holmes leaned far back on the crude stool and exclaimed, "This day in Scotland is adventure for the ages."

He leaned forward from his nearly horizontal recline, emptied his beer mug and added, "This beverage as well."

"I have never before felt myself such a tourist," muttered softly Wells in English. His words were delivered with such seriousness that it precipitated such a raucous laughter from Holmes and I, that Wells, not immune to self-mockery, was unable to resist. So occurred our first moment of joy as 11th century men.

There was food and fauna, unknown to my eyes, plants of all sorts that sat on roughhewn planks as inexpensive décor and advertisement of potions, for no one within view could read.

"Watson, do you recall the butterfly now confined to Dartmoor moor?"

I nodded.

"You have not written of it one of your entertainments. It would make an interesting read."

I remembered the events of Dartmoor and made a mental note to put it to print when we returned to London.

"No matter, it can wait," Holmes said as if he read my mind.

"Many of these plants and small animals here displayed are extinct in our time. It is a pity. Take for example, that short reddish green shrub with five leaves. It has not been seen on this island for centuries. I must talk to the exhibitor."

Holmes wandered off to converse with the man.

"Wells," said I switching to English, "you have an unimaginable treat before you. Yet you look as if you are about to enter a dentist's chamber of horrors. There is food and drink and look, games to watch."

"I am not sure how I convinced myself to have volunteered myself and my machine for this expedition," Wells said, emphasizing the last word so that it sounded like a tropical disease.

"You mention a dentist office and I think of the anesthesia found there. I wonder if this is not in reality an opium induced dream, a condition I must sadly reject as I do not consume narcotics.

I am forced therefore to honor my word and accept reality and do my utmost to make this a success, although I remain unclear on exactly what our goal is."

I hesitated to repeat that this was Holmes' investigation into the truth behind the MacBeth play. We had stated that as our goal before departure from 1894 at the beginning of our voyage, and he had accepted it gracefully as a white lie to someone who did not need to know the actual truth. I feared that had he known that the entire venture was little more than a whim, a pre-Victorian Victorian folly, he might have conveyed us at all haste back to 221b.

We watched the games. I was pleased that Wells began to show interest, and we moved closed to the competition.

Holmes joined us a few minutes later with the plant of five leaves in hand."

"Why on earth did you buy that item?" Wells asked.

"It was the only item I knew for certain was harmless."

Holmes spoke in English, having heard other foreign languages being spoken at the fair.

"I saw that the seller of plants was also the local blacksmith. It was obvious from his upper torso and the horse and ox shoes overhead. A normally suspicious person may mount one horseshoe, but not the half dozen he has displayed. The plants are mere attraction for the fairer sex and her husband."

Wells said nothing, but his admiration for Holmes' skill was evident.

"Blacksmiths speak with and hear everything. Unfortunately, our is not young, and he mishears many conversations. He is but another marginal witness in our pursuit of truth. I must make bricks without straw at times. The smith relayed to me in a staccato voice indistinguishable sparks of truth and opinion, each flying from his mouth like the beating sound of his massive mallet."

"Brevity is the soul of wit, Holmes," I admonished.

"In brief then, the plant's expense was payment for information on the witches."

"Witches?" I guffawed.

"Here at the fair?" Wells asked more rationally.

"Yes."

Wells and I stood there expectantly.

"They are named Morag, Judith, and Ruth. They have a booth here as well."

Wells and I frowned in unison at the improbable statement.

"Testimony from your deaf witness is suspect at best," Wells argued."

"I agree," admitted Holmes. "It is not Bradshaw's."

Holmes paused, then added "I have seen them myself. The women concoct and sell herb and lotions, and various potions. Their wares deserve a closer lock."

"Who would purchase from witches?" Wells asked before I could mouth the same question.

"People follow my impossible-improbable axiom in their daily lives to the point that it is as unrecognized as the air they breathe. The seek medical treatment wherever it can plausibly be found, locally by necessity, at a fair like this if the opportunity presents itself. Those is pain will seek relief where it may be found. If the alternative is continued illness, they will seek assistance from witches.

The fair locals must have considered us crazy, possibly witches ourselves, but were either too courteous or too fearful, to state it in our presence. In hearing my Scots accent, more than a few may have reconsidered, assuming no doubt that I was having one over on the southerners, for they tipped their cap and shot winks at me from time to time.

We strolled around the grounds of the fair, our target the booth of the three sisters.

"They are young," Holmes said, as we approached.

"And not unattractive," Wells inserted.

"They will make better witnesses, I think."

I addressed one nonchalantly by name, Morag. As luck would have it, I'd guessed correctly. Morag was shorter and finer than the other two sisters, themselves not taller than the average. Black hair and dark blue eyes, a perfect, if diminutive, example of national clan.

The others, red haired both, one slightly freckled and eyes of sky, the third sister with eyes of freshly turned loam. The trio were sturdy of bone and teeth. I regret describing them in phrases equine, but I am not a writer of dime store romances. Indeed, had they been men, the same terminology would have been appropriate.

The sisters' clothing however was in a state that hovered as indescribable beyond qualifying as coverings. Despite their paltry rags, each sister was a gem.

I spoke with Morag of unimportant things, while Holmes and Wells were enraptured by their separate, respective pursuits.

Holmes was amazed at the offerings on display.

"Many of these are extinct, viewable only in old texts, while others I are completely unknown."

At last, I was able to drag them away, claiming that we had need to meet the King, one way or another.

I directed them to the men's competitions, where a nearby dais had been erected, presumably for royal viewing of the matches.

"These are precursors to our own Highland Games," I said proudly.

"Anyone and everyone is in attendance. It is a double edged sword, of which many of those will be present as well. We are able to blend in but we need to stand out., if you truly hope to meet MacBeth," Wells said bluntly..

"We must participate and make ourselves desirable guests if we are to cross into the castle. We must be seen as quarry not as a hunter.

"Well considered Wells," Holmes agreed.

"We must be invited in as we cannot enter through force   hat do you propose?"

"Archery for me, for it is the art of the lower class, a role that is draped on me here with my lack of linguistic knowledge

Watson will wrestle, that is self-evident."

I straightened to my husky height in agreement

"And I will be the poet, for that too is a competition," Holmes proclaimed, eliciting laughter from Wells and I, for while it was a part that fit as well as peccary gloves, he claimed the role with such confidence as to ring pretentious.

Our sports thus divided, we proceeded to compete and excel in our meets that our goal of being guests in the castle was achieved

Pencil and paper being precious commodities I will waste neither in describing each competition.

Suffice to write that we succeeded and were met by the king himself.

CHAPTER EIGHT Invitation to MacBeth's Castle

They came seeking us, three victorious strangers. What a sight we must present to the local inhabitants present at the fair. Two of us old, in a year a few decades past the first millennium. The world is still young. The first crusade is decades in the future, few of those alive today will live to hear of that event. We are old, but in good health, with strong teeth and the soft hands of the non-peasant. We were curiosities in a world lacking them. We could offer them entertainment, or more. We had presented ourselves as chroniclers, learned in the healing arts and dabblers in stagecraft, magi far removed from the tainted arts of the distaff side.

The natives are young, oh so young. Macbeth is 27 years of age, the same number of years as Wells.

MacBeth, young, with the healthy complexion of a warrior king in his prime. No shadow of villainy does he wear. This is an era where strength and rapidity in thought and action were equal if not superior in result than studied reflection.

And if not, one had little time to learn, else cede way to a successor.

The king and queen were a vibrant couple, well paired, comely in appearance. One thought of a lion and lioness harnessed invisibly by their common dynamism, ready to defend one another, or to leap in tandem upon presented opportunity. They lived joyfully in their youthful and powerful existence, oblivious to the future libel that comprised their lives in countless British libraries. They would not hear the yet unborn slander that would insult them from innumerable stages.

The King congratulated us on victories.

"Never have I seen such performance as from you three. You are as three warlocks. Evil comes in that number."

"Neither Magi or the pope would agree, sire," replied Holmes.

Not warlocks then, for we have enough of sorceresses without importing from the south. You profess yourself troubadours. I find the worst are pushed by the best this far north. What talents do you have that will not make howl our wolves in accompaniment?"

"Fresh stories not yet heard by myself, let alone your majesties."

"That is indeed magical."

"As to the wolves, I will not sing, for then you would take me as one."

"This one, does he not speak?" MacBeth asked, pointing at Wells.

"He speaks English, which to our ears, is indeed the howling of a beast, one less than a wolf, sire" I replied.

MacBeth was not one to abuse his tongue with politesse on his inferiors.

I understand that the southerners are too occupied in finding kings to replace those who die to exert themselves with claiming new kingdoms. Is it Harold who sits or lays?

"It is Harthacnut who reigns in England sire," I said.

"For how long? England loses it land and leaders at an appalling rate. Most recently, I hear talk of a confessor coming to England. Surely my messengers must not speak your language as well as I pay them. The thought strikes me that you are here on errand, emissaries to beg me in advance to assume leadership of a spinning kingdom. 'Twould not a tempting offer make."

"I could not imagine a Scotsman of this era more suited sire, but alas, my commission does not extend that far. In fact, my only commission is to entertain with stories my fellow man, elevated or prostrate."

"A vocation then?"

"A worthy word for a man of action. My offer is not a crown, but chronicles worthy of a princely hearing."

"Which sort of stories bring you?"

"Tales that delight or frighten, according to the hunger of the crowd. I can recount the histories of vampires and werewolves and other stories of such ilk"

"I have heard nothing of what you speak."

Holmes realized his mistake.

"Then it will not bore you my lord, as these are not local oft told tales. Likewise, I can bring laughter to the castle with escapades of identities mistaken and assumed.

During this time, MacBeth's consort had remained as mute as Wells.

Lady MacBeth regarded us innocently, calmly. She did not perceive that we, with 200 years of indoctrination, perceived her as the epitome of feminine evil. The queen was courteous, open, welcome to what must have appeared to her clear blue eyes, as deep as a loch, her hair raven and flowing. I digress. Holmes' frequent counsel to observe at times runs counter to results. This was such a time.

In short, Lady MacBeth must have seen us as a worthwhile curiosity, worthy of time in a world without clock or museum. I was continually impressed by Holmes' command of what to him was a foreign language, having though him restricted to the King's English and a few distant, obscure tongues.

We three visitors emitted the bizarreness and rarity of the far East for our hostess and her eyes flicked from one to another of us as the evening progressed and tensions dissipated.

I must now apologize to the Lady, centuries late. She gave me no cause to doubt her innocence, or to see her in any light other than a woman of her time. There are worse epitaphs. Holmes has remarked on several occasions, and here I paraphrase, that I miss the forest for the trees, whether they are firmly planted of shuffling forward from Birnam Wood.

"Come this evening to the castle. I am a good host, and my wife will be find amusement at three more kings, or witches. We have a surfeit of both kings dressed as fools and fools outfitted as royalty. And witches galore. I shall hear words but decline your magic. I will remain protected as one Scotsman may vouchsafe the two Englishmen."

The queen nodded her approval us to MacBeth and the two left us.

The games ended, the fair closing, we gathered, found our way to the castle of Mac Bethad Mac Findláech, and gained admittance.

CHAPTER NINE In residence at the castle

Lady MacBeth was protective of her husband. They were as well matched as a set of spice shakers from the best silver mason in London. By all appearances, she was in love with her husband and he with her. I suppose it is natural to love strength and competence. Violence encapsulated both in that era. Holmes was at times perplexed by love, but he respected competence.

Was competence controlled passion, I wondered, or was it simply distilled and best kept bottled for special occasions. For such days as an authentic warrior king might face every day of his reign. Perhaps today itself, nearly a millennium before tomorrow's yesterday in the snug confines of Baker Street would be such an occasion. Nasty, brutish, and short was apt description for the times.

We viewed the castle, then an operational resident fortress, as busy as any seat of government, and not a paid exhibit for tourists.

We dined with the royal couple, and Holmes began the conversation by commenting on the impressive nature of both MacBeth's home, but also his realm, exemplified by the display of goods and military prowess shown by the Scots. I had not seen Holmes so effluvious.

"It must profit immensely your renown and coffers, and bring pride to the attendees. One booth," Holmes noted, "had an extensive array of goods, herbs and libations, the equal of which we have not seen in all of our travels. It truly was extraordinary."

"Goods sold by evil," Macbeth replied quietly.

"What mean you, my lord?"

"Your description fits only one trio. They are named Judith, Ruth, and Morag."

"It is the very same, sire. You know well the look and name of your subjects," I said.

"Each time I see them I shiver, albeit it be as hellish warm as today. I sense in them something what others call otherworldly, but to my nostrils they are too far this side.

They are the wind that cools the heated brow and the tempest that tosses about the coldest hearted stalwart.

I would advise you to steer clear of those sirens, but I sense in you three an appetite for danger, though I would not wager which of your three has the greatest hunger."

I translated as best I could for Wells who sat quietly, trying his utmost to not appear the dunce.

Lady MacBeth continued the warning.

"The trio seeks too much from the powerful."

She cast a glance at us, perhaps including us as another threatening triumvirate.

"What is that they seek, my Lady?" asked Holmes. MacBeth answered.

"What many fools seek."

In the pause that followed what could have been issued as a riddle, Wells responded, "Wealth?"

To my translated answer, MacBeth replied,

"The greatest wealth. Power."

"They have latched on to my husband like lampreys."

"My queen describes them well. I find their presence a reminder that vigilance is the price of a crown."

"A price that Duncan forgot to pay."

"Indeed. They are an unwanted inheritance from the dead king. He hung on their every word. Methinks at time they see me as their legacy, and not affairs as they are."

"Until they turned on him, as they will on you," warned the queen.

"To kill a witch is bad luck. And three?" MacBeth stated.

"To not erase the clan is bad reasoning," was the feminine retort.

I was amazed at how readily they discussed murder before guests. Despite her cold words, I did not think of her then as an arch villain of the eleventh century. If such had been the case I would have set it down. Alas, I had nothing.

"It was they who killed Duncan."

"Nay, it was the drunken servants. That night is but a blur, and yet one whose bright ending I cannot forget. Never was the wine as strong as that evening, and never was the morning so painfully sober."

"That was the past, what's done cannot be undone," Macbeth stated, putting an end to the subject.

"They are as innocent as you or I, and are unlike any witches I've spied."

"Is that many my Lord?" I asked.

"The three fill my game bag."

MacBeth looked at us quizzically.

"Let us talk of merrier things and tonight let us listen to happy stories from our worldly. If tonight is well received, we would enjoy a longer recital tomorrow eve, a play would not be unwelcome. Title it as you choose."

That evening Holmes recounted one curious tale after another, and I offered a few myself. Our daily life became to the royal ears marvelous inventions of what could never be.

Would Wells experience the same incessant disbelief and amazement in his trip to future? He had told me that he intended it to be a one-way journey, leaving the unpleasant present behind forever.

It was late in the night; the summer sun had taken itself to sleep while Holmes continued to disperse amazement. Finally, the three of us were applauded, and dismissed, for surely the king said, we would require time to rehearse for the following evening.

A command performance, an event to which Holmes was accustomed, was to me a singular honor, from a genuine Scots royal no less. Clean hands or not, I was still ecstatic with the invitation.

Once in our quarters, we reviewed the night's events.

"I think we are no closer to resolving your riddle, than when you tossed MacBeth across our living room," I said to Holmes.

"The couple is of their time," Wells said.

"What more needs to be done here? We can leave tomorrow morning."

"And the play?" I demanded, reluctant to leave a promise unkept."

"The witches are central to the play," Holmes said, his tone indicating to me that he was thinking aloud.

"You are repeating a line from the actor in Stratford," said Wells with a yawn.

"They are essential to the play; therefore, they must be real. Witches disguise themselves with humanity. Shakespeare is more clever than he is given credit."

"Really Holmes!" I exclaimed.

"Which play, and which witches?" Wells said.

"I must be tired to be talking this way about nothings," he added.

"I must agree Holmes, you are fixated on witches," I said.

"I dare say you are part sorcerer yourself, with your bottomless satchel, full of gloves and tobacco, and I expect a proverbial rabbit.

"It is no more miraculous than your medical bag."

"There are no witches, Holmes," Wells said with a note of finality in his voice.

"It is not a fixation on witches, or a figment of imagination precipitated by our time traveling."

"What then?" asked Wells.

"It is you who are fixated on the word, witch. They are organized. They are witnesses by their testimony. Remove the word witch from the description of the sisters and what have we?"

"Women?" I responded.

"Yes, women. They are also authentic actors in the drama."

"In Shakespeare's play."

"Yes. More importantly they appear in this real-life drama. Their disguise is a method for the weak to act powerfully. Men underestimate women, but they fear and respect these women, all down to a monosyllabic noun. They are as deserving of our attention as the King and Queen. We are all in costume here."

"We need to write a play, Holmes", I said, resigned to the task.

"It shall be child's play for we have studied at the feet of Shakespeare himself. We are educated, erudite."

Wells spoke from his position on the large floor mat that served as his bed

"You are an odd pair. Someone should scribe a book of you two."

"Watson here has done so."

"You have more than just the one story that brought me to your door? It was by happenstance that I happened to read it in a café. Someone must have left it behind."

"A few," I replied. "I publish regularly."

Wells recognized his faux pas.

"It is not through lack of interest or quality of writing on your part that I am not a regular reader. Each farthing is a screw, a rivet, an electron in the maw of my own mechanical manuscript."

Holmes laughed.

"Wells you are as ignorant of the adventures of Holmes and Watson as anyone now alive, save your two companions. Irony has placed you here in our earliest adventure, where no printing press exists to herald it. It would translate well to a play, but not this one, I'm afraid."

"What use will I be in this stagecraft?"

"You may play the fool, or the uncouth foreigner. Which tongue will you speak in your idyllic future?"

"A point I have not yet considered, I admit," replied Wells, accepting graciously Holmes' retort.

"Tomorrow, I will be as mute as a mole, a veritable troglodyte, however erudite."

"Not at all. Your lines will be phonetic. You may observe and take notes. I take you for a quick learner, you can learn the script and speak as best you can. Be loud in lieu of precise. The audience will comprehend."

"It must be brief, but long enough. A tapestry of amusement with just the best bits showing," Wells offered.

"Excellent," Holmes supported.

"An overture?" I suggested.

"The very thing. And remember, comedy. Brevity is the soul of wit, is it not Watson, and humor its cousin. This castle does not ring with laughter. Now to work, he said as he scribbled notes.

Holmes, Wells and I had little choice but to do a quick montage of plays seen and read, where laughter was the sole goal. Never had a trio struggled so mightily on a show that would be staged but once. We combined various pieces of recent and distant experiences, along with plays we had seen or read. We accomplished what no playwright or group of playwrights had ever done; we stole from the future. The squares were stitched into a meaningful, comedic performance. It contained witches, murders, ghosts, servant, annoying children, magic, stumbles and pratfalls.

Here to the best of my recollection is the summary of the original version of the play not MacBeth, but the play for MacBeth, entitled The Three Beths.

Three maidens: Lesbeth, Betty, and Lizzy, are the daughters of a bumbling servant, who was so busy that no one knows how he was able to father children. Three traveling strangers, each with an annoying difficult to pronounce name arrive at the inn run poorly by the father, only with the aid of his daughters.

Throughout the play the father calls his daughters Beth. The father proclaims, 'I meet enough strangers, that in my home my rules, and one name for all is a rule.'

And if you had been blessed with a son he is asked.

He would not like his name.

The daughters complain among themselves.

The guests, three fathers and sons are enraptured with the sisters, but confusion occurs as they must all referred to as Beth or William when the father is around, which is often, given that there are only three actors, and a bear skin draped over a chair that serves as a fourth actor when the scene is too difficult. Otherwise, the actors wear masks to portray the numerous characters.

The visitors are passing annoying, our father passing strange. And we are passing our lives into old age. Gold flows naturally to youth and we are young. War does not call us, but we must call it. Our lives are triple trouble if we act not. Our own sons will spring from our gray admirers (or their sons if they pass the audition).

And each of our eaglets will not his name share with his cousins unless Birnam wood come here.

Let's meet again tomorrow and plan for our future happiness before age stales us, the sisters agree.

We prefer the sons, who while not yet broken, they can bridle.

Next day, the three fathers are killed in a fearful accident and the marriages followed uncommonly soon, attended by three ghosts, who for some reason remain restricted to the use of either Beth or William.

CHAPTER TEN Second Night in the Castle

We dined at the king's table before we performed, a kind gesture on his part.

The food was bland but plentiful. I hoped it was not a harbinger of our own evening offering.

Wells called my attention to the arrival of Morag and her two sisters.

MacBeth noted their presence as well.

"The witches are in attendance."

"My lord is accommodating indeed," Holmes said circumspectly.

"The porter has let them in, for he fears their wiles, more than he quivers before my wrath. They are harmless to the man who plugs his ears."

"Why not replace him?"

"He is the best of a bad lot," MacBeth replied.

I nearly spilled my drink at the expression.

"He is a useful pawn if the need arises," the queen added.

"I think the sisters will find your play of interest."

"Why is that my Lady?" I asked.

"They are three as are you."

"The competition and preening has moved indoors from the fairgrounds," added MacBeth.

The conversation moved on to other topics, and soon it was time for us to deliver our entrée. Holmes rose to address the king.

"For tonight we have as title The Three Beths. If you enjoy the play sire, you may give to it any name you choose, including yours. If not, you may call it Forgotten."

It had been left to me to speak the falsetto roles, while Wells mouthed admirably his assigned lines. The audience was generous, our accents were beyond English, but at the end we received applause.

I remarked after the performance that MacBeth had retired from the great hall early, only touched one drink and yet appeared overly affected by it.

"Did you notice he claimed to see one of the ghosts we conjured. Did he call it sire? I confess to having the hearing of a blacksmith at that moment," said Holmes.

"And after the play his behavior was as that of a different man."

"He spoke as if he were rehearsing his own play," I said.

"What did he say?" asked Wells, who had not understood a word of Macbeth's Gaelic.

I repeated as best I could recall.

"I am as a father, in charge not in control. The porter's door unlocked by Beth and his love of drink."

"It was gibberish in any language," I commented.

"They drive him mad by degrees."

"Who?"

"I noticed that his drink was brought by the porter. Is every employee drunk?" Wells asked.

"Or is he in league with the servants who murdered Duncan?"

"This place reeks of intrigue despite the humor of our work. It requires more than an evening's laughter to dislodge a staff of betrayers. This is fertile ground for an English playwright or Scotland Yard, but neither as yet exist."

Wells remarked what did exist.

"The night is still young, the play has energized me Holmes, and the three sisters are as yet unaccompanied."

CHAPTER ELEVEN The company of women

Holmes glanced at his glass, then gazed deeply into it.

"There is no opium within a thousand miles, no cocaine within thrice the distance and yet...passion is the root of all."

I wondered if the strange behavior exhibited by MacBeth had claimed a new victim.

Holmes raised his eyes to us.

"The witches remain?" he asked.

Wells exploded.

"Witches don't exist!"

"War exists," Holmes replied in gentle reprimand.

"Really Holmes, one must draw the line somewhere," Wells retorted.

"Witches or not, this trio troubles us. It is they who constitute our focus."

"Why?" Wells posed quickly the difficult question.

"Let us examine the facts and then the possibilities. They are central to the story in the 1600s and here in the more distant past. They were Duncan's confidants and seem to have a similar if diminished role with MacBeth."

"One madwoman is common, a triplet less so."

"I daresay that a trio of madmen is extraordinarily common. We have only to consider ourselves," Wells commented wittily.

"Point taken. And to that point, I am confused when I am with you Holmes. It is not fever from our time hopping, for I felt this way the first time we met."

"It is often thus in the middle of a case Wells. I am left to my own devices and when I miss a critical point, Holmes will explain all after the fact."

My words appeased Wells, or perhaps it was Ruth, who at the moment waved in our direction.

"They beckon," Holmes said.

Holmes had complained repeatedly about the lack of newspapers in general and absence of personal columns in particular in both of the centuries that we had visited. I leaned over and told him in English that the present situation was the best equivalent.

My experience in these matters far exceeds that of Holmes, and I therefore took lead.

Wells suggested that we divide and conquer but almost immediately reconsidered and that our safety was only to be found in numbers, three to be exact.

I directed myself toward Morag, while Ruth attached herself to Wells, and the third, Judith, the saddest, wisest, and most hardened I judged with reason, to Holmes.

I asked Morag what she thought of us. She ridiculed us as unarmed men who believe themselves powerful because we play the fool for a foolish king. So we were either truly fools, devils in disguise, or men with wealth enough to play the fool. She called herself foolish as well, for one does not mock fools or devils.

I smiled at her forthrightness, for in her world there were situations where nuance needed to be jettisoned.

I noticed that Holmes and Wells were in conversation as well, drinking and laughing. I could not imagine what Wells and Ruth were discussing, but I supposed it was the universal language.

I grew more comfortable in Morag's presence, and her attractiveness compensated for the limited range our conversation could take, for she was indeed poorly educated. Whether she continued to think me fool or devil, she could not have conceived of what I was in truth. I sensed other eyes watching us and felt a certain sense of security in knowing that we were under surveillance.

Morag lived part time with her father, who, she repeated several times, would likely soon die, and she would be, while not rich, for that was unfathomable, an owner of a few fertile acres. I nodded.

Morag persisted in detailing to me the crops and herbs that she raised. I must confess that my vocabulary in Gaelic did not extend to where I understood all she was saying. She identified that some returned more than others for the same space. These were essential for the sustenance of both her and her father, who would likely not see another spring. But she could not see the future, he might die sooner.

I recalled Holmes' statement about the widowed mother's insurance claim shortly after our first meeting.

"You cannot see the future?" I asked, steering the conversation from flora.

Morag laughed. "You ask me a silly question."

She laughed again then became serious.

"Why do you ask me such a question? Can you?"

She smiled and moved a bit closer.

"Tell me then strange English-Scots man, what the future holds." The 'for me or us' was unspoken but not unheard.

Morag poured for me a cup of wine, but I had drank enough that evening. The preparations for and the play itself had tired me, and it began to show. I brought the cup to my lips but knew that more alcohol would put me to sleep.

I walked her home soon afterward. I flinched in embarrassment when she placed her dirty, calloused hand in mine. She smiled in the fading light, her face orange in the glow, my own crimson blush hidden in shadow. I reached out to accept her friendship.

CHAPTER TWELVE Comparing Notes

"Why not go back and see the murder itself?" I asked.

"This adventure of yours would have been the work of an hour if we had done so," Wells said.

"That is not how I work," Holmes explained. "This jaunt of mine is an exception, but I shan't go that far. Macbeth knew us not at the fair; therefore, we have not taken your proposed action. The talented fraction of Scotland Yard has accused me of meddling. The machine would compound it to no end."

"It would be a one off, a matter of mere moments," I tempted.

"Shall we advance a few years and negate Hastings? Surely a conquest is monumentally more important than the death of a minor Scots king. It is a shame that Mycroft has not accompanied us for such stagecraft is his forte. Or shall we reverse further and step on the head of Eden's serpent? All whom we meet today are tomorrow dead."

I questioned Holmes logic.

"Our own today, how does that differ? Our work in tomorrow's London, is that equally meaningless?"

"Tomorrow's London is our rightful jurisdiction. We have duty there."

"And our duty here?"

"The past is a foreign country, Watson. Yesterday is not within my purview. I accept my limits."

"We have come this far and now what? Are we three wise men to leave with our precious gifts still in hand?"

"We cannot take the law into our own hands," said Wells. If we could, if we did, to what end? What verdict?"

I considered his question.

What sentence could we impose? Wells added.

"On whom?" Holmes asked.

"Why on MacBeth of course. Or...he is but an instrument of Lady Macbeth?" I suggested

"We are in not in school, dissecting a play for high marks."

"We either act or not. Blast it," I said, "we are all Hamlets."

"I created my machine as a lifeboat, not as a battleship," Wells stated.

"If you had not lost her, and come to us for assistance, you would have abandoned your time for..." I began.

"For a better future," Wells supplied his motive.

"Whichever ship you reach will be little different than the one you are preparing to quit."

"You are wrong."

"I doubt it."

"You must be wrong. Humanity cannot continue on this path, for we shall surely destroy ourselves."

"Crime and stupidity are constants, and you seek to change them," Holmes said.

"I am not Don Quixote. Mankind will change them, and I intend to be there for the unveiling."

"If that is to happen, it will occur only if you are the last survivor of an extinct species."

"Our brain advances us; our emotions govern us. It is a tug of war that only increases our destructive capacity. It must reach a decision point."

"We are living flesh and blood, not metaphors. This is real life, despite its incredulity. We are not living a fantasy."

"One day I will kindly ask you to elucidate the difference Holmes," Wells responded with a smile."

The conversation was nearing an impasse, as politics and religion are wont to do.

"I agree with Wells, we have no power over the couple, either singly or paired. She is the power. Like a toddler he sips from the cup she offers him. He is not the first to be misled by his consort."

"These people have had their chance. Are we to remain here in yesterday and attempt to right every wrong?" Wells pursued.

"She is not a comma in a history book," I said.

"She is a free individual?" Wells modified his question, "As much as any human is free?"

"Yes," Holmes replied for us.

Wells pivoted towards me.

"Life is not an endless series of mulligans that we can referee. She is free to choose well or poorly. Am I wrong? This is beyond the Good Lord's desire. None of us are omniscient."

He winked at Holmes.

"The courts make an effort," I offered.

"She is the court."

"You choose not to intercede Holmes?"

"I choose not to interfere."

"We must investigate."

"I admire your passion" Wells said.

"But?"

"You overstate our ability. One false word or suspicion and we ourselves would sleep in unmarked graves."

"You are correct of course Holmes."

"There are lives as precious as these that we will prolong in our way, in our time. The machine can return us to where we must and should be, Watson."

"My machine is ungainly but nothing on Earth can outrun it," Wells said proudly.

"Your device has a tinge of evil about it. It is a telescope that lets one observe a child about to drown, far offshore and beyond reach.

We are machines as assuredly as the time machine. More or less well-oiled than your temporal conveyance, we follow the direction of forces we do not comprehend. I do as I think. It remains a mystery as to why I think as I do."

Is there a difference I asked myself as I wondered which of my two companions was more obstinate and colder. I suppose that physicians can be equally dispassionate.

"Did you understand Ruth?" I asked Wells.

Wells grinned. "Enough, I think. Who comprehends women? I am seeing her later. Perhaps we can communicate better during daylight."

"Is that wise?" asked Holmes.

"Women are wise," Wells commented, refuting his early slight against the distaff half.

"They adapt. They persevere."

"They overcome?" Holmes supplied.

Wells shook his head.

"No, they do not overcome. They survive. Their survival ensures our own survival. I wonder if Eden wasn't simply an argument against complacency. I don't fancy myself enjoying being a gardener, with the fig leaves, what?"

"Or less," I remarked.

"Women find a way to survive, building a life in this barrenness would be a stretch."

I took umbrage at the image Wells portrayed.

"We have been building lives here for millennia," I informed him.

"Sorry Watson, it was just you talk of Morag and her herbs and plants, eking out an existence, wishing her father into an early grave that made me speak so unkindly. MacBeth and wife prove your point that life can be pleasant."

"She is a woman, as strong and as weak as those in our own time," Holmes said.

"Times change, humans don't."

"But they will," Wells argued.

If any men had less claim to ignorance as excuse, it was solely and jointly our trio.

Marriage to us is their instrument of revenge on MacBeth. They have failed to bend him to their will, for how long they have tried I can only guess. Drugs are their method to ensnare us.

"We are means to their ends?" asked Wells.

"Chattel is the word you seek," Holmes replied bluntly.

They interpreted The Three Beths as a group proposal. I chose to provoke them into action. They must realize, as we do, that we will not remain under MacBeth's roof indefinitely. When we depart, their intention is that it be six and not three that turn their backs on this realm."

I have no desire to remain any longer than it takes to satisfy myself with my conclusion. I confession, private or before you would be sufficient. That will not be the result. With a choice between victory and seeing Victoria again, I choose modernity. Let us depart tomorrow midday, as soon as Wells is ready. Alas, it's a pity. And the trio? They are the root cause of this bloody business."

"The three will return in the morning and we will verify the truth. It is only a matter of hours."

I chuckled at Holmes slicing time, given our current power over it.

I reconsidered Holmes words, thinking I had misheard.

"Trio?" I echoed. "Surely you mean pair."

"There is not trio self we three," Wells agreed.

A moment later he asked, "The sisters? Our three Beths?"

"Yes."

"How's that again Holmes? The women?".

"Yes. They are the genuine villains in this misunderstood play.

"It is a short slip from murder to marriage," I quipped, thinking this a joke.

"They have staged it so well that they have fooled the bard himself. This is no slight on him for he is six centuries distant, while we ourselves have brushed against the principals themselves and nearly been tricked.

The three Beths are truly skilled magicians, if not certified witches. It is much the same."

Clapping his hands together slowly, Holmes said, "I applaud them.

They are master manipulators. Oh, Mycroft would marry any of them, if not all three. The women employ poisons, soft and hard, and hallucinogens to direct their victims to commit these crimes. They are as skilled in costumes as any professional actress, talented in their own way as a Hardy Street chemist.

They drugged MacBeth as the three of us noted. I have seen enough drug usage to recognize the symptoms and behavior.

I saw Ruth pass a tainted cup to Wells, as Morag did to you."

"I did not drink the wine," I said.

Holmes nodded.

"Judith passed presumably the same concoction to me. I drank mine.

"What?" Wells and I exclaimed in unison.

"My experience with and tolerance of opium and cocaine provided a degree of protection. I had provoked them into action, although from their perspective they saw the play as a public offer of marriage."

"I do not understand," Wells said before I could.

And I have provoked them.

I was flabbergasted. Their conclusion about the women was so wrong, yet delivered so nonchalantly that they might have said the two plus two equals sixteen.

I recalled Wells' statement of a previous day that unmanaged evolution was a two-way street and that there was no guarantee that progress was more than a temporary stay. Had Holmes reverted to an irrational creature during this voyage? Or was I too dull to comprehend their logic?

"I will explain," Holmes began, lighting his pipe. Had he no end of tobacco, I wondered as he continued his illumination.

"The sisters are convinced that Macbeth has wronged them singly and by family. Land theft, preventing an advantageous marriage, the details are unimportant, they had replied in the only way that the powerless can; silent acceptance, obsequiousness, and then revenge.

They drive MacBeth as if he were a machine through the use of a plant, extinct in our day. They drug him and he kills Duncan, or they do the deed, and Macbeth believes the murder was by his hand or another. It does not matter, as long as the old King is dead, and the new King is there for the sisters to manage.

In a culture given to fantastic beliefs, in a land regularly plunged in long term darkness, such shadows result in myth becoming fact and the most powerful of personages act irrationally. A few drops of potent on food or in wine and you have murder. Witches are real in one sense, overrated in most. Our own hallucinations are evidence of their presence and impact."

"Uneasy the head that wears the crown," I quoted.

"With a nudge from the three chemists, MacBeth hallucinated, acted, and..."

"Clearly. This accounts for ghosts and delusions. Revenge is as addictive for these three women as..." Holmes trailed off.

Wells filled the void with a voice filled with disbelief.

"You theorize that they target us?"

"The evidence supports the theory."

"They will not stop of course," I stated.

"He is their puppet on the proverbial string. Ghastly," I added.

"And Lady MacBeth?" asked Wells.

"The same," replied Holmes.

"The plant or potent you theorize is provoking paranoia, a new word for an ancient malady."

"I bow to your medical skill Watson," Holmes complimented.

"Then our case here is concluded."

"Women scorned!" Wells exclaimed, disgusted but unconvinced.

"We have come all this way for that. Your uncovered truth is disappointingly tawdry Holmes."

"Crime often is," Holmes admitted.

Wells withdrew. He walked to a corner of the room where he contented himself with cold food and tepid drink. A few minutes later, Wells left us to perform his periodic inspection of his machine. I admired his dedication but not for the first time I wondered why such constant attention was required. I suspected that he would visit Ruth to question here. How he hoped to do that in pantomime, I was unsure. Wells took my revolver with him, as ever since our run in with Ian and his gang, it was too dangerous to venture unarmed far from the castle.

Holmes and I sat before the small fire, like us its flame unnaturally quiet. Long moments passed before I referenced the obvious.

"The case is solved but not resolved."

Holmes remained silent, no indication that he had heard me in the confines of the tiny lodgings. We sat, wordless for more than an hour. I was about to repeat my statement where Wells burst in.

"Come quicky, something is wrong with the time machine. We need to return immediately, or you will need to acclimate yourself to this day's pentameter. The automated return gears are chattering."

"Can you disable it?"

No, it is a failsafe in case I was unable to operate the time machine when I arrived."

"But you are not alone."

"You altered my plan with your folly, Holmes. The machine's components are all integrated. If the failsafe is out of order and it hasn't been used, what else is suspect? My fear is of what I don't know."

We stood in unison, only in time to see Wells nearly swoon before us. He gathered himself before total collapse. A wild look came into his eyes, as one may observe in patients at Bedlam.

"Witches!" he snarled.

"What have you done to my machine and me?"

In an instant his face returned to normal, and he was once again in our shared reality.

"Watson, Holmes, there is something wrong with the machine. We must leave now or never. I fear that we have overextended it with too much usage. Let us return!"

Like his invention, Wells' hold on the present was tenuous.

"Witches!" he repeated before collapsing in our arms.

"I warned him! The sisters have made a second attempt with Wells, who being younger and monolingual, was seen as better quarry. We wrote our play too well, Watson. If they had wanted his death his body would be chilling on the stone floor of this chamber. They are as skilled as you in pharmaceutical craft."

"It is time to return Holmes," said I.

We had no time for farewells.

We gathered what few possessions we had and headed to the time machine; the night sky lit only by a sliver of moon. Between the two of us, we managed to transport the inventor to his malfunctioning device.

We settled into the machine, Holmes at the controls.

"As our cabbie is incapacitated, I will drive," he said dryly. Before he pressed on any lever, he looked straight ahead, considering if he had overlooked any alternative.

"If we were to idle here, hovering like a hawk near the shore at a spot in Devon, suspended between surf and tufts of vigorous grass, wind and waves frozen from their unpausable motion, would that not surpass any narcotic dream? There in that permanent moment, oscillating ever so minutely twixt present and past, or future and unremembered yesterdays.".

He sighed with regret.

"Let us return. I have learned enough, and our case is complete if not resolved. Morag was the key, her patch of green her laboratory, her father a likely guinea pig."

I shivered at the thought of way lay ahead for us if we were forced to stay behind.

"I have no need to see how this particular play ends, for it will end as it does for all mortals. This wonderful invention you have led us around in Wells," he said to the unconscious inventor, serves to illustrate the passage of time and how futile it is to seek to prevent it. Death has followed us into the past as surely as we will meet him in our futures.

We have faced more determined enemies, but never one so insipid and immediately effective. As to the problem at hand. Our first problem, eh Watson?"

And with that, he pushed on a lever.

CHAPTER THIRTEEN Back home

As we slowed and then stopped into our present, I took a final look around at our conveyance. By this time I considered our Time machine a faithful if exhausted companion, and I knew that we would not share further adventures. Normal time would be fine with me for the remainder of my days.

We returned to London by train and then to Wells carriage house by team and hansom. I daresay I may have caught of glimpse of ourselves as our trains passed each other near Cambridge.

Holmes and I left Wells with his invention, Holmes promising to have the undercarriage of the time machine removed, returning the device to Wells' original design. Thus encumbered, it would serve Wells within the confines of London.

Before we separated, Wells said, "It will be with regret that one day I will read of your obituaries. Watson informs me Holmes that is will be your second time mourned.

While we still shuffle along on this mortal coil," he continued without sarcasm or irony, but in complete sincerity, "I will regard fondly our voyage to the past, for in it lies the creation of a recollection I will cherish forever."

I had mixed emotions upon reaching 221b Baker Street a few hours after we had left eight hundred years earlier. It was confusing, the sense of travel lag when venturing through time was a feeling I would not miss.

The next day my mind was clearer, and I was able to reflect on our fantastic journey. It seemed unreal.

I held in my mind the fossil of a shell, an impression on another's life, a solidified yet vacant memory. It was a dream which however unbelievable did not fade as the day progressed. Now I regard this purely internalized photograph as a vibrant colored image of life, faintly false at the moment of capture, more so as seconds of time dripped by. In apology to the reader, if there is one, if you are confused by the above paragraph, I have succeeded in expressing my own state in the days following our return.

"It was she, Adler, that woman," Holmes would say.

He had his enigma, and now I had mine.

I looked around at our lodgings as if I were a first time visitor to a museum, each item an artifact of a time long or recently past. Each item was a time machine with an unalterable destination. Was this truly our quiet, unassuming lodgings on a quiet street in peaceful 1894 London?

Who would have need of truth, either yesterday or tomorrow? Veracity is overrated; I could hear my friend state unequivocally.

Melancholy afflicts me, yet Holmes is unaffected. As a medical man, I wonder if time travel has its own illness, like sea seasickness, which affects some and spares others.

Holmes is unaffected, so I may suggest my hypothesis to him, perhaps he may even write a monologue on the subject. No, no one would believe it, and would conclude that we are a mad pair, or trio, if Wells' name is mentioned.

No, Holmes is almost joyful, returned to this, his era, to his beloved cesspool overflowing with miscreants.

The gory past was best left there, no match for the vitality and violence of modern London. The past was as boring as Bristol in winter.

I wondered what became of the women. Had I attended school with their descendants? Had they had issue? The thread of poor families is easily broken, lost by the vicissitudes of time and chance.

"Will you work with Wells again, Holmes?" I asked.

"I think not. He has his future, and I mine."

"It is the same for me, I think. One such adventure was sufficient for me."

"Agreed, although the trip was not without its rewards."

"We have not earned a guinea. Those given to you by Mycroft you spent."

Holmes began to light a pipe but changed his mind and returned it to the mantle, where it sat next to the adulterated folio of MacBeth. No word was uttered, neither critique nor praise for the late playwright, whom we had spoken with only days before.

"I am surprised that you choose not to smoke, given the quantity you consumed on the case."

It really had been a sight to see Holmes puffing away like the Flying Scotsman, immune to the mocking name of the English dragon given him by the locals.

Holmes remained silent

I wondered what he had meant by rewards and asked him.

"There were several Watson. I was able to retrieve this sample of what until now has been an extinct plant."

"The one the witches' used to create all this mayhem? It is poisonous. This is madness."

"Perhaps it is their last act at distance, but to have brought something back from death, albeit a plant, while some may consider it witchcraft, I classify a miracle. No matter, here it is and here it will remain."

He reached for his pipe but again stopped short.

"In addition to reviving a dead plant, I did my part in learning a near dead language. Yours as a matter of fact."

"Gaelic?" I asked. "You took it upon yourself to learn Gaelic. When?"

"During our trip."

"Which trip Holmes?"

"Why this most recent adventure, Watson. I took the machine back to modern Stratford, journeyed to Scotland and enrolled in a private three-week course from a native speaker. It was fortunate for us, as I was able to conduct the time machine when the need arose."

"You did this before convincing Wells and I to return to 1041?"

"I know you well Watson. You enjoy complaining about adventure almost as much as adventure itself. One is spice, the other meal."

"And Wells?"

"He enjoys dining, as wells he should."

"You learned to drive it in one lesson? Amazing."

"Well, actually more than one Watson, quite a few. I did run short of tobacco back then, you know. Perhaps you noticed? It was for shared benefit of the three of us, for I need chemical stimuli for my brain as other men require their own form of sustenance."

"That was how you knew about the hidden control!" I exclaimed.

"Little is hidden to the dedicated observer, Watson. I have offered this advice on numerous occasions. I was gone for weeks, mere minutes to you."

Holmes reached a third time for the pipe and this time he did light the tobacco nestled inside.

"I do wonder though if my numerous trips contributed to the poor machine's breakdown. No matter, we are here safe and sound. All's well that ends well," he said as he straightened the mistreated copy of MacBetth in its place of honor on the mantle.

POSTSCRIPT

Neither Holmes nor I will see MacBeth, or any of Shakespeare's works in the same light again. Whether this is a blessing or a curse I have yet to determine.

As to this journal, I cannot in good faith christen this a case, but will do so anyway, for I cannot publish it. It would be ridiculed, mocked, evidence presented for my confinement to Bedlam. I cannot bring myself to burn it.

I have promised Holmes and Wells not to publish this story during our lifetimes. Holmes feared being branded a fantasist, a creator of fiction. Such a result would bring no new work, and in this I agreed.

Wells and I had our own, no less important reasons for remaining silent. In the back of our minds I wonder if we didn't entertain the possibility that we might be thought witches ourselves despite the rationality of modern London.

Therefore, I will permit this narrative to see the light of day when the three of us no longer do so. This is case to destroy a career, and I will send it forward, into the future, where like a child's potion, its effect will be harmless to the sender.

Wells has lent me his model, with which I will send this sole copy into a future, a future that the inventor assures me will be a better world than this. If he is correct about what is to come, neither Holmes nor I would find ourselves content in such a pacific land. Holmes has said more than once since our return, "There is no time like the present."

I have one final errand to complete at the library.

87

I've placed a small camera in the model time machine, another of Wells' inventions and if all goes to according to plan, the device will return with an image of a present I will never see except in one photograph.

If the machine returns not, I will need to reimburse Wells for his model and camera and likely stand him a round at the Grey Horse, where we are scheduled to meet shortly. I think that I will stand him a round regardless.

EPILOGUE

I removed the book from the small red leather seat of the toy. The cover was without mark, neither title nor author's name appeared on it

A slight click, followed by whirling sound, emanated from the gift-bearing machine and in a second it vanished. I was distracted and only glimpsed its disappearance, so startled and intrigued had I been by its inexplicable arrival and its paper occupant.

I brought the book closer to my eyes and inhaled the smell of fresh paper as I opened it.

There on the first page in large sharp print was 'THE ADVENTURE OF THE WITCHES' BREW by John H. Watson, M.D.'

I sat in the London Public Library, reading the same book you have just finished.

The original book, as I said, exhibited no sign of age. Aside from the paper of its construction with its absence of atomic radiation residue later proved by test; it appeared a well done fake. The ink, while old fashioned, readily smeared as I studied the book.

You may find its contents credible or ludicrous. We choose our own beliefs and path.

As to me, I was a prodigal son, one of many I suppose although Shakespeare did not concern himself about us. It is my own pride that had brought me so far from home.

In another era, I'd have hidden in Paris, but I am not one for foreign language, British English excepted. Paris furthermore, has become overridden with foreigners "doing Paris", to the point that native Parisiennes are those in hiding. Things turn out. For the best or as intended I cannot say.

People do not change, or so one says. If people lived as long as cities do, I've little doubt that the proverb would not have been uttered. For despite the best efforts to protect and preserve, today's London is not that of a century, let alone centuries ago. For every conservationist, there are numerous progressives and developers. It is a war of attrition, and the futurists win.

We imagine that we control time with our detailed schedules and precise timepieces, but temporality tramples our temporary truths, as King Cnut humbly proved.

All things must pass, including Roman walls, Norman castles, or the unremarked passage on an itinerant American.

And so, this prodigal son had a purpose. I returned home to find my own way. In time.

I chose to publish this book in my native country, for reasons that I will not disclose. Aside from the American spelling of certain words such as 'apologize', the story you have read is as I have received it.

I returned to England recently for a long delayed private tour. I took myself to the same pub as Watson and Wells, the Grey Horse, and had a pint myself, and reread the unique story which you now find in your hands in book format. Past, present, future. Does any of us ever have enough time?

Larry (Roger) Cardenio
2024

www.ingramcontent.com/pod-product-compliance
Lightning Source LLC
Chambersburg PA
CBHW031855170626
46807CB00004B/1734